JOURNEY

TO

A HERMITS HAVEN

DOUG MCPHILLIPS

Also, by Doug McPhillips:

NOVELS. AND ALBUMS
From Darkness to Light
Awake to My Gutted Dreams
The Sword of Discernment
Santiago Traveller
I Prophet: towards 2030
Masters at my table
The Guru of Jerusalem
We Are Me Upside Down (Auto-biography)
The Wicklow Way
The Adventures of Ace McDice,
 Stretch Deed & Moonshine Melody
Instant Karma & Grace
The Credo
Reflections of an Old Man
A Writer on the Rock s
Reincarnation of the Assassin
Master of the Arts
The Songs, not the Singer
To Whom It May Concern
Masters of Introspection
The Rise and Rise of a 4th Reich
New Shouts from Old Branches.
A Camino Guide Book
Country Camino (Album)
Santiago Traveller (Album)
Soul Fact.(Album

Doug McPhillips December 2024 ISBN.978-1-7636983-5-2

Keywords appearing in this novel in italics are in the author's first person.

Contents.

The life of a solitary man is told here by the teller of this tale.

A hermit is a person who has withdrawn to a solitary place for a life of religious seclusion. Hermits like to live alone, in the woods, on a mountain, or sometimes in modern living. They live in a city without hardly ever leaving their apartment.

Hermits are sometimes called Anchorites, although the two are legendary based on location. In Christianity, an anchorite was someone who, for religious reasons, withdrew from secular society to be able to lead a solitary life. An anchorite traditionally selected a cell attached to a church or near a crowded centre, turning inward to meditate, pray and fast for long periods, whilst a hermit retired to the wilderness for many reasons, not all religious.

This little work tracks the life of a hermit who took an inward journey to find himself. I leave it to the reader to determine if the main character in this story is a hermit or an anchorite. The lessons he learns and the peace he secures help the reader decide whether you, like him, are one of a solo kind whose mission is to live in this world but not of it. The story herein is entirely a creation of the mind of the teller.

Authors comment.

CHAPTER 1.

THE CAVE

I observe life as a pilgrim on the road to my happy destiny. It was not always so, as I strove with all my might to fit into the pattern of what the world had to offer. I had shifted many times to become what I thought life was about. As always happens to humans, life twists and turns to bumpy roads and smooth roads as we stalk the rocky way towards our ultimate destination. I thought I had it made for a time, the answer to the riddle through power, money, and prestige, but that would come crumbling into the dust. Early in life, I learned to follow my mother's advice: 'Love many, trust few, but always paddle my own canoe.' It seemed I was destined to fall into many traps as I did my utmost to shape the world to my liking.

I often believe that I had made a connection to a God of my understanding whom I trusted and prayed for guidance to, even when I was at my lowest points with depression, a sense of despair and alcoholic behaviour. When the worst of my nightmares engulfed me, I began to drink even more as a bandaid to get by. When no answers came, I often turned to another woman's arms instead of going to God. The outcome of this behaviour only made my life a living hell, and I found that the problems in my life were worse. I was forever attempting to discover grace and peace of mind. In the worst of my nightmares, I recognised that I was powerless over alcohol, people, places and things. I could not rule the world, and I could not let the world rule me.

Like all alcoholics who become sober and come to terms with the insane way of my former life, I soon realised I had been a square peg trying to fit into a round hole. I examined the path of living sober and realised I belonged to that one to three per cent of the world's population who did not fit the patterns of what the material world had to offer. Through much tragedy and living in dark, shadowy places, I realised that I was born to be a hermit. I woke up to the fact that I lacked the bounds of worldly living and needed to retreat into some secluded cave to meditate on the eternal spirit I was given to believe God created all things. I had concluded that the answer to my riddle for living now was to hand over to that infinite intelligence of all creation that I call God. I didn't need to define anything; I opened myself to whatever came up, trusting this powerful force as my guiding light to the path I was always meant to follow.

In my time of recovery, I learnt to trust in the slow work of God through prayer and meditation. I live like an anchorite of old living according to religious philosophy, retreating to Churches and religious memorial locations to meditate and ask for guidance. However, my belief was more akin to the structural template of what I was taught to believe and not the way of one who had retreated from the world. So I abandoned myself to the Higher Power I came to believe in and accept within the depth of my heart as undefinable. This new understanding gave me the freedom to be guided to its will. I was no longer an anchorite living a spiritual way of life but a hermit conscious of the reality of my existence and awaiting the healing power of this power greater than self to open up the way for me to live by.

Only after a long period of walking the world as a pilgrim did I come to pass into a new haven of awareness. I now relate what I knew to be accurate and what transpired then. It was like a dream state that I was in, but it was natural to me at the time, and it became a guiding light to inspire others and led me along many pathways to be and do the will of this undefinable God-head. I was awakened to an out-of-body experience that could not be explained in the real material world. I will relate that here for our mutual spiritual benefit.

I awoke in a large cave with many Aboriginal drawings. Aboriginal drawings depict a story of the way of life of those early cave dwellers. It was then that I concluded that the earliest of humanity not only lived in caves but retreated there to meditate and, with artistic mastery, create pictures for the telling and benefit of future generations—a legacy, if you will, for humanity to this very day. Looking down from the ceiling, I observed a flat wall face with light appearing from a cave entrance beyond. Not far from the door were walls on either side, with people chained hands and feet to the walls, with only the view of the flat wall ahead, which appeared like a giant screen to them. They had no other way of knowing what was beyond the cave, for they could not look around to look outside, dependent upon the shadows that appeared on the screen-like wall ahead to assume what it was that they were seeing.

I became aware one of those chained to the wall was me. So I moved inside my body and became one with the other people chained to the wall. Thus, My mind entered into a period of former memories, for it was not the present that I was perceiving but the past. Then, a person to my left asked, " What do I see passing by on the wall before me?" I explained that it was not on the wall but a shadow from the light coming in from the cave entrance behind us. As I was working from my memory, I began to explain that the image I had concluded was that of a man riding a horse-drawn wagon. Then, I began to relate a fact of my childhood, in the early 1950s, when the local baker delivered bread to the village people by horse and cart. Then, another image appeared of a large vehicle carting a load of timber logs. I then related that this was similar to the trucks that left the sawmill at the edge of my village with timber destined for far places for building houses, piles for peers on docks for ships and transporting goods by sea. So this led to many questions, and each of those pinned to that wall wanted to know what I had learned about what was beyond the walls and outside this cave. Each, in their way, had a viewpoint as to what they pierced the shadows represented, and many were in disagreement with what I perceived as the reality at the time.

In God's good time, not mine, I was given to find that without rhyme or reason, I was released from those chains and made my way out of the cave into the light of day and the reality of the present day. I soon forgot the cave and the experience I had there for a time. For it was that I had grown to manhood for better or for worse and became engulfed into all the world had to offer materially, including every pleasure known to man. Little thought entered my head of a higher being that created all things and His Godly purpose for humanity. I was destined for power, prestige and what I perceived as my destiny. I had amassed a fortune in gold and silver, traded in goods and services for the benefit of the many, married and educated my children, and to the rest of the world, had it all. And yet, I was not content with my lot in life, believing that my hard work and fortune were all I needed. I became discontent, thinking that there must be more. There was an itch deep inside me that I could not scratch, and it took a calamity to occur. I lost all, including my family, and I collapsed into a state of depression and total desire. Then I cried out to God for help, and the answer was given slowly in his excellent time, not mine.

I had come to a mystical side of myself that could not be expressed in words or through worldly deeds, a cause that could be fulfilled only by the spirit that was central to the candle that burned within - a candle that, to me, was a symbol of life itself, a flame that burned at a deep level, projecting light into the darkness. And in the flickering awareness, I could almost hear a message: "Exist; stay alive; survive." Here, for the first time, I was learning about my true nature, being aware of my body, my mind, and the true spirit within. I had come from darkness and had tried to clutch too tightly to the past when my worldly claims engulfed me. Yet here I was now, surrendering my all, falling moment by moment into that surrendering and risking falling into the unknown, falling into the fearful dragon's mouth of self-acceptance, with the fear of falling into a pit of darkness where the dragon lived, where there was no light, only darkness, of weeping and gnashing of teeth.

I was coming to a vacuum and was surrendering and letting it sink into the marrow of my bones. I knew it was time again to fall into the bottomless pit where the dragon lived, to descend into the dragon's mouth, in my mind, and there I would find a lotus flower. There, falling into the hell of the bottomless pit, I would reach a vacuum of nothingness (no-thing-ness). In that state, the dragon would turn into a lotus flower of creative ideas – the womb of rebirth.

I determined to adopt an accord of consciousness with every human being with whom I would come in contact on my outward and inward journey: a journey of understanding, a journey of nature being both cruel and kind, of being as vigilant as a female serpent within my inner being on the pathways of my life, and as innocent as a dove. A freedom nothing bar death could take from me – my freedom of choice for living. I knew within my heart of hearts existed a Sword of Discernment, and I longed for an outward expressive symbol of this inner need and courage. I would let go of my inner turmoil and take a journey of the spirit – my spiritual heart expressed in a tangible symbol. I could think of no better way than the way of St. James, the apostle, whose symbol was a real Sword of Discernment; the sacrificial cross of St. James, the fleury fitch, whose sword blade signifies the sword of a warrior. I would follow the path of St. James. The Moor-slayer, on The Camino Way, where I would lay down my burdens and walk the traditional Way that so many pilgrims had walked before me.

It was then I felt that I knew the outward expression I sought would manifest into the sword of St. James. Like the Spanish who fought and conquered the Moors so many centuries ago, their vision of the Saint on a white steed advancing before them holding aloft a fiery red sword of Santiago leading their charge and taking them to victory, I, likewise, would venture forth on the road to Santiago, leading ever onward with a courageous cry, to the quest that pierced my heart.

I would walk The Camino de Santiago! Whilst I would seek a symbolic sword as proof of my journey, I knew that my Sword of Discernment would be more than merely a sword. I knew I would express in words the cry of my heart, the link I had to my past journey. My current turmoil is in my spiritual quest. I would venture forth with hope and confidence despite the night of the soul. I did not yet know the events that would unfold due to walking my Camino. The thought of a new dawning after the long night gave me the courage to proceed. The night was darkest just before dawn, and I ventured forth despite the sword that pierced my soul.

I had taken an inner truth of honesty to myself, an open-mindedness and a willingness to grow, a willingness not to worry, acceptance, and belief in living with whatever comes my way. I began to relax then, to allow the coil of the wound-up spring within me to trust in God without definition. I knew it was not the old ways of strength, enthusiasm, leadership and dogma that would project me like an arrow towards some designated target. Instead, it was to be a slow road, one day at a time, moment to moment, using the coiled spring's spiritual thread to unwind, unravel and let go to gain inner calm. I was learning to use no force, to let the force within take hold, allowing time to heal and grow. I knew I needed to go with the grain, as an artist working with wood, in time, knows. Often, in the past, I ran against the grain, and the result was splintered wounds. I was running now with the inner river's flow and going with the current in open water. I knew a gentle rudder movement would keep me on course once I understood and accepted its drift.

So it was armed with the knowledge of my need to let go and step out there that I made my way to Spain to walk the Way of St. James, the Apostle of Christ. I had only a small backpack, a change of clothing, and toiletries. I set forth with no map, even though I knew not where the adventure would take me. However, out of fear of not finding a place to rest my head, I carried a small tent and sleeping sack, but it was not far into my pilgrimage that I disposed of those, preferring to let fate provide food and shelter along the Way.

I had set out to let go of all my past feelings that I had been holding on to in preference of coming to that meditative state where one becomes at one with the Way, and ultimately, The Way itself became me.

I'm walking the Camino,
on the way to Santiago,
Yeah, I'm leaving here today,
Because I'm on my way,
walking the Camino,

Walking the Camino,
Walking the Camino.

CHAPTER 2.

THE WAY

"The Way is for the most adventurous and curious of free-spirited travellers. I passed through uninhabited wilderness and traversed towns, villages and urban cities. The Camino was more than just a walk in the woods for me. It inspired a novel, a book of prose and an album of songs that might not have happened had I not taken the journey. I have completed another novel and a new album of songs inspired by two more Camino journeys."
– Doug McPhillips.

My first Camino in 2013 was to prove awe-inspiring for me. I was there to let go of the feelings of pain and suffering over the past decades where tragedy had entered my life. I had suffered much over the slings and arrows of outrageous fortune. So, on this first Camino, I experienced a serendipitous event that would change the next decade and onward until this very day.

It is when one is in a dark space, a depressing hole if you will, for I could not rise above the sense of despair and hopelessness until I set out on that Camino. About 500 kilometres into my pilgrimage, I met a rock and country folk musician. We had been walking with some other pilgrim youths at the time, a band of brothers with me, and I was the old-timer in their midst. Someone produced an old guitar hanging on a wall in the alley we were staying in, and the rock musician began to play and sing a ballad he had written. The song touched my heart, and I announced that I had written a poem that could be interpreted as a ballad. I was encouraged to recite it and got applause from the audience. The rock musician said little, but on my return home to Australia, he emailed me asking if I would send him my lyrics as he wanted to put them into music and record them on his band's upcoming album. As I had no chorus for it at that stage, I wrote back that I had no chorus, and until I did, I would keep it. Instead, I sent him two other poems, one he recorded on the album. Then, once I had a chorus down, I sent him the lyrics. He soon put it to music and recorded it as a ballad on the following album. I had a lightbulb moment when I could write songs. Over the next year, I wrote and recorded ten songs with professional musicians, wrote a book of poems and published a novel. I had been down the dragon's well of darkness to where the dragon lived, and what emerged when I hit the bottom was not a dragon/s mouth but a lotus lower of creative ideas.

I began building my website, www.caminoway.com.au, record-ed more songs and wrote many books. This process continues to this day. My hermit retreat has become a hive of creative ac-tivity. It is not a place to hide and contemplate the universe but a garret for the creative mind to tap into the muses that guided me.

On my return to the world, I began many projects and achieved material success again. Puffed up with pride and self-worth, I returned to the Camino. This time, not to let God, but rather to fall into the arms of a lover once again. The women, as had al-ways happened in my previous relationships, turned me into more pain and heartache. I had not learnt the lesson of the daily habit of turning to God, preferring the embrace of women. I re-turn to Australia a ragged man, a shadowy figure of little worth. The experience led me back into rehabilitation and a long, slow journey back to health.

After learning the lesson, I returned to The Way for the third time. I was mindful of the errors of my past pilgrimages and resolved to walk the Camino for my soul search rather than that of worldly pursuits. This time, I walked nearly 1200 km through rain and sleet, wet to the skin and freezing most days., At night, I removed my wet clothing, soaked my wet boots, and placed them in front of a log fire in a vain attempt to dry them. It was useless as it rained for the next 5 weeks, and I continued to live in wet clothing.

In the following decade, I came to write many more books and two more albums of my songs. However, the sense of not getting to the depth of my soul's purpose in life still alluded to me. So, as time passed, I decided to return to the cave where my transcendental state of mind had once led me to a new way of life. I was recalling those men and women chained to the wall in that cave. I walked the arid desert of the Northern Territory in Australia to find the cave again. So, entering in, I took up a lotus-like crossed-legged position next to the wall where the light shone in from outside the cave. I prayed for guidance, and soon, I was in a trance-like state and ready for the mission I had set out to achieve there.

Looking around the cave, I noticed only one of the men who had been there years before I left. It was my duty to explain myself, recounting all the works, prompts, and ceremonies I had been fortunate to be involved in. I retold my Camino journeys, how I was given by some miracle to be guided to the muses to create my songs and write of matters spiritual for those willing to read them. The man previously on my left, who once asked me many questions, was more content to live now. I had so concluded that he was drawing near to his time to make his way in the world or be destined like me to take up the life of a hermit. Many of these people plied me with questions as to what they were visualising in the shadows that appeared on the wall next to me. I was delighted to explain what they saw, having returned to the world and observed what had happened over the previous decade.

I then felt compelled to explain that what I had come to believe and learnt to accept was the spiritual journey we are all destined to take if it is God's will. Only some people would be given the privilege to leave the material world in search of that desired ritual essence that the anchorite and hermits would ultimately pursue.

I began explaining what I had perceived in terms as best I could to benefit my captured audience.

Imagine a large circle drawn on a piece of paper representing the outer edge of our known world. Then, picture a dot in the middle of the circle, which we may call God. Then, suppose we have billions of radii emulating from God in the middle to the outer edge of the earth's circumference. This may be construed as the path of all humanity who follow the dictates of their own free will away from God in pursuit of worldly rewards and not those of the spirit plan that God has ordained for humanity to do. It is not hard to accept the journey of those who turn back towards God, letting go of the shackles of worldly needs and wants in preference to doing what God has planned for us in the first place. You are still chained to this wall and do not know why, but the plan is being revealed to you. Trust in the slow work of God, for your time, will come to return to the world again, but you will learn to be in the world but not of the world. Your destiny for a time will be that of an anchorite on some spiritual mission or that of a hermit destined to live in isolation until God calls you to action.

I then felt that I had said enough, for I had my mission in life to attend to. I had my cave until I received my next calling from He, who knows everything and will lead me to the promised land if I believe, meditate, listen, and learn my call to act.
To develop one's personality means fidelity to the law of one's being…Fidelity to the law of one's being is to trust in this law, have loyal perseverance, and have confident hope, which is, in short, an attitude such as a religious-centred man should have towards God. It can now be seen how portentous the dilemma that emerges from behind our problem personality can never develop unless the individual chooses his way, consciously and rationally. The casual motive- necessity- and the conscious moral decision must lend strength to building the personality. A man can decide to go his way only if he holds that way to be the best. If any other ways were held to be better, then he would live and develop that other personality instead of his own. The fact that convention always flourishes in one form or another only proves that the vast majority of humanity does not choose their way, but convention and the collective mode of life at the cost of their wholeness.

It's a small wonder that only the chosen few embarked upon this strange adventure from the earliest of times. Had they been fools, we could safely dismiss them as mentally private per-sons. As a rule, these personalities are the legendary heroes of humanity, the very ones who are looked up to be loved and worshipped, the true sons of God whose names perish not. They are the flower and the fruit, the ever-fertile seeds of the tree of humanity…They tower up like mountain peaks above the masses of men of quiet desperation who still cling to collective fears, beliefs, laws, and systems and boldly hold on to their way. The man in the street has always seen it miraculous that anyone should turn aside from the beaten track with its known destinations and strike out on a steep, narrow path leading into the unknown. Hence, it was always believed that such a man, if not crazy, was possessed by a demon or God.

What is it that, in the end, induces a man to go his own way and to rise out of unconscious identity with the masses as out of a swathing mist? Not necessity, for necessity, come to many, and they take refuge in convention. It is not a moral decision, for we decide for convention nine times out of ten. What is it that inexorably tips the scales in favour of the extraordinary?
It is commonly called vocation, an irrational factor that destines a man to emancipate himself from the herd and its well-worn paths. Vocation acts like a law of God from which there is no escape. The fact that many a man who goes his own way ends in ruin means nothing to one who has a vocation. Anyone with a vocation hears the voice of the inner man: he is called. To be called is why the legends say he possesses a private demon who counsels him and whose mandate he must obey. The original meaning of " to have a vocation" is " to be addressed by a voice." The clearest examples of this are found in the protestations of the Old Testament prophets…In the place of the inner voice is the group's voice with its conventions; collective necessities replace a vocation.

In so far as every individual has the law of his life inborn, any man can follow this law and become a personality, that is, to achieve wholeness....Only the man who can consciously assent to the power of the inner voice becomes a personality, but if he succumbs to it, he will be swept away by the blind flux of psychic events and destroyed. The tremendous and liberating thing about any genuine personality is that he voluntarily sacrifices himself to his vocation and consciously translates into his reality, which would only lead to ruin if it were lived unconsciously by the group.

One of the prime examples of the meaning of personality is the life of Christ obeying the inner call of his vocation. Jesus voluntarily exposed himself (in the temptations) to the assaults of the imperialistic madness that filled everyone, conqueror and conquered alike. In this way, he recognised the nature of the objective psyche, which had plunged the whole world into misery and begotten a yearning for salvation that found expression even in the pagan poets. Far from being expressed or allowing himself to be suppressed by the psychic onslaught, he let it act on him consciously and assimilated it. Thus was world conquering Caesarian transformed into spiritual kingship, and the Roman Empire into the universal kingdom of God that was not of this world. While the Jewish nation was expecting an imperialistically minded and politically active hero as a Messiah, Jesus fulfilled the Messianic mission not so much for his country as for the whole Roman world and pointed out to humanity the old truth that where force rules. There is no love, and where love reigns, force does not count. The religion of love was the psychological counterpart to the Romans's devil worship of power.

The example of Christianity best illustrates my previous abstract argument. This unique life became a sacred symbol because it is the psychological prototype of the meaningful life, that is, of a life that strives for individual realisation absolutely and unconditionally. Well, may we claim to be soul-natural Christians.

The deification of Jesus and Buddha is not so surprising; it affords a striking example of humanity's enormous valuation of those heroic figures and, hence, upon the ideal from personality. The idea of personality is one of the ineradicable needs of the human soul.

As great personalities act upon society to liberate, redeem, transform, and heal, so the birth of personality in oneself has a therapeutic effect; it is as if a river that had run to waste in a sluggish side-stream and marshes suddenly found its way back to its proper bed or as if a stone lying on a germinating seed were lifted away so that the shoot could begin its natural growth ...*

* Carl G. Junf, M.D. 1875-1961 Swiss Psychiatrist
 The Development of Personality.

CHAPTER 3.

PILGRIMS CONCLUSIONS

I had come to the other side of my personality, and in my calling, a new vocation came to me in my risking all to step out into the great unknown. For some time, I had hidden away like a hermit, seeking peace of mind to get my mental health back again. In this seclusion, I risked stepping out into the great unknown. I packed a knapsack with a set of clothing, no plan, no map to guide me, and no clear direction for where life would take me; I headed to the Pyrenees Mountains to make my way across northern Spain and walk the Camino Way. I set out like a lone wanderer, determined to let go of the past way of life in search of some spiritual home.

It was a form of consciousness and belief to enter into a presence of mind, to live the truth of who I was and what I was to become; not an artificial self-will but consciousness to bring synchronicity of no longer being an artificial person in an artificial place. I had historically lived a religious philosophy that no longer applied to me. I found myself believing in a power geared to the self, the spiritual values of handing all my life over, and having the faith to think I was being guided. As it happened, it proved to be true.

It was not just the poems, the songs, or the plethora of written words in novels that excited my creative imagination; it was the coming of a mystical side of myself that could not be expressed in words or worldly deeds. It was a cause that could only be fulfilled by the spirit central to the candle that burnt within. A candle symbolises life itself, a flame that burns at a deeper level, projecting light into the darkest recesses of the soul. As I tramped the Camino, I kept up that flickering awareness that could almost be heard in the words of Master Lao Tzu, reportedly uttered by him in 406 BC:" In breathing stillness of body and mind, an inner flame is born." So I must keep it burning in mediative walking through my guttered dreams.

The Camino led me to my inner soul, breathing a lotus flower of creative ideas. The tragedies and sadness I had suffered taught me life lessons, for nothing important comes to materialisation without suffering. To me, it left my body coiled and tightened with depression and anxiety, and panic followed, claimed me and engulfed me. I had been running around a pit of hell, which only caused me more significant anxiety and, ultimately, complete exhaustion. In my physical pain, my mental torment and spiritual death, I became aware once more of the real me. At the time, I did not have the strength or bodily health to endure a short walk, let alone consider climbing great mountain ranges, although I did so in my dreams. I had lost everything I thought my life was about: family, business, home and wealth. In my desperate need, I had turned to lovers when I should have turned to the God within, for lovers brought with them their pain in mine. However, they did get comfort in my agony; it was my ego illusion in their mystic love rites, in brief moments of the enchantment of the Goddess within, that ultimately just brought me disenchantment and even more illusion.

My saving grace was ultimately making an effort, a day at a time, to walk the road less travelled, to climb great mountain paths and hidden valley crevices. Whilst on a journey of inner truth, I was now mindful of the dangerous ground of more worldly desire, which I knew would lead only to chaos deep inside. The words of another great Chinese philosopher entered my being: "We ought not to live the afternoon of our lives as we have lived the morning of our lives," It seemed like a sign of my way of learning to let go.

So, the new way of the inner spiritual journey is still unfolding. I am still between the old way and the latest, but I was learning to let go of my ego notions, letting that inner core of being take hold. That something from nothingness (no-thing-ness) where I now believe the universe began, where something that came from nothing is my God. For the first time, I was learning to cut through the reality of everything that made up my former life. Now, I am becoming free to discover more within myself, that enlightened ability to judge and act with wisdom. In truth, I was to find my inner nature of discernment as a tool to carry like a staff of a pilgrim of old, a tool of action in my uniqueness, and a brand of reason and responsibility. I now have the choice to go with the flow, be friendly and easy, and be enlightened with the good karma of creative ideas. To pursue or not what I wish to become to realise what was, is and always will be. All I have to do is tap into the source of all and channel it into creative works for the good of all concerned. This is my world now, my work for the benefit of those in the present and much more, those future generations whose spirit, needs and aspirations must be guided so that they may have good reason for living and hoping in our troubled world of good versus the not so.

I have now concluded, after many tramps over Hill and Dale, many songs written, poetry expressed, and stories told of life experiences lived, that I have tapped into the creative source of an enlightened ability to live according to the dictates of my conscience. I recognise the beauty that lives within me as being in every man. Each of us on this earth, irrespective of our living circumstances, must be on to whatever we pursue with our God-given talents. Some are born to recognise their creation abilities for the common good, and some of us, like me, have them thrust upon us when we are open to receiving them. It became a journey of understanding nature being cruel and kind, of the need to strive to be happy, but simultaneously being as vigilant as a female serpent on my life pathway, as gentle as a dove. It is the freedom of living that nothing short of death can take from me, freedom in the choices for living. I am living the dream with outward expressions of my inner need and the need for my courage to prevail. I let go of my inner turmoil, venturing forth in spirit and understanding, initially expressed in my Camino poems, songs, and stories.

The Way of St.James on my Camino was the catalyst to opening up for me the need for self-sacrifice, for it was no longer about Doug but the journey back to the way of the spirit. My duty from here on is to give an account of my stewardship. This Pilgrim of The Way followed the path of St. James on the Camino at times, where I lay down my burdens, walking the way that so many Pilgrims had walked since medieval times. The Templar Knights of old had ventured on 'The Way' at the express wish of the Pope at the time, protecting Pilgrims like me from harm and material hardship. It took their journeys of The Way to venture forth 800km to Santiago. I had followed and led in a courageous cry to the quest that pierced my heart, for I was seeking my home and didn't know it all along. All along, I was searching for love and through much pain and sorrow, I would find it in the cry of my heart, in the tears of my soul, in that every constant pursuit of endless ideas and actions, leading to an ever-onward ultimate cry in the piercing of my hearts expressions of love for the God of my understanding. The night of the soul, I had faded into a new dawning. The first light of the crack of dawn broke over the city of Santiago.

The sun's early morning rays shone over the Cathedral steeples appearing above the sea of grey building silhouettes emerging from the darkness. The constant pounding of my feet on the cobblestone echoed in the silent city streets as I walked, stunned by the beat of my heart—the sound of a different drummer. Upon arriving at the Plaza de Obradoiro, the large open Plaza outside the Cathedral, I was greeted, hugged and kissed by many of my fellow pilgrims I had met on my arduous 800 km trek of The Way. I felt like I was with a quiet, loving group of angels and entering a seventh heaven. In my body and the shadows of my mind, I felt the presence of many medieval pilgrims who had gathered and kept a vigil in the Plaza, awaiting our arrival to join the midday Pilgrims Mass ritual. The Cathedral was packed with two thousand Pilgrims for this Sunday service where the spectacle of the Botafumerio, the 'smoke belcher,' that swung back and forth connected on pulley ropes and worked by eight monks in unison kept the large incense dispenser swinging. I remembered that it was installed in Medieval times to cover the stench of the multitude of unwashed Pilgrims who attended the Mass at the height of pilgrimages, done in homage to the reported resting place of the bones of St. James below the altar.

The sweet smell of incense whiffed throughout the Cathedral as the belcher spread its smoke above the crowd of Pilgrims gathered there. The incense symbolised clearing the world of darkness, cleansing the souls of this wayward and world-weary pilgrim and those present.

The Camino had been a letting go of a past life and darkest hours for me, and now I was in the light to live, really live. An ancient copy or scroll of one's Camino was the traditional thing to obtain at the end of one's Camino after the celebration of the Pilgrim's Mass. I walked the few blocks to the Pilgrim's office with my fellow Pilgrims to receive my 'Compostela Credential,' the proof of completion awarded to those who made the required distance on The Way to Santiago. It was my third certificate, having walked the 800 km from St. Jean-Pied-de-Port on the French side of the Pyrenees to Santiago twice and the Lisbon to Santiago Portuguese route once in the past six years. It was not the 100 km on foot to Santiago, nor the 200km on bike or horse qualification, which is the qualified one attributed as a certificate of completion. That in itself is an anti-climax to having walked the whole Way. However, I have three Certificates on my Office wall at home as outward proof of having done the distance and a steady reminder of the outward and inward spiritual aspects of my journeys on my Camino.

My last Camino complete, I wandered the streets of Santiago in a semi-trance, listening to the laughter of people in sidewalk cafes, meeting by chance Pilgrims I had met along The Way and once more being with them in peaceful surrounds, listening to the music of the street, enjoying the pleasures of food and just sitting in quiet contemplation watching the world go by.

Reminders of other pilgrims I had met on my first Camino drifted back, and thoughts of our last supper together and our fond farewell, as we parted for all points of the compass drifted back. We had promised to catch up sometime in the future. I knew it was unlikely to happen back then, for that moment of joy, pleasure, and parting was over. I was on a new path now, and I jolted my mind and the feelings of my heart back to the present. Another night's stay had me up at dawn wandering the streets alone, mindful that the pilgrims now arriving I had never met and were unlikely to either. I had decided to look inside the Cathedral before the madding crowd of pilgrims and tourists descended the entry stairs and spilt into the open Plaza at the front of the majestic structure.

At this early hour, the staircase to the back of the altar was tourist-free, so I climbed the small steps to the statue of St.-James, touching the golden form and placing my hands on his shoulder, asking for blessing from his spirit in the great beyond. I descended to the vault below the altar to a silver casket, which reported holding the bones of St.James. Whilst this had been my third visit to the vault since my first Camino in 2013, I did not believe the bones within the crypt before me were the actual remains of St. James. There were too many conflicting myths and no facts to prove the real ones. However, if I am wrong in my assumptions, I knelt and prayed before the shrine again, as I had done on two previous occasions.

In truth, I knew the remains (bones) had been discovered 800 years after James had reportedly preached devotion to Christ on the Iberian Peninsula between 40 AD and 44 AD. St. James' bones had also been misplaced for 300 years before being returned to the Cathedral in the sixteenth century. In the quest to uncover some truth of St. James' spiritual message of Christina's zeal being carried out on The Way, I once more walked the city searching for symbols and signs of his existence and mission being fulfilled on the Iberian Peninsula in the early years that followed the death of Christ the Saviour. Apart from stories of his leading the troops into battle 800 years after he walked the earth here, there are no official facts of his actual existence, his time in Spain or his ability to ride a great white stallion with a fiery sword overhead; leading the troops into battle against the Moors, some 800 years after his reported existence.

According to archival records, St. James' mission commenced not long after the death of Christ, when he agreed to sail to the Spanish Peninsula to walk The Way North, preaching the word of his Master. His most famous biblical quote is: "Faith without works is dead." In a more modern vocabulary, " Action speaks louder than words" was James's message. Apart from attempting to convert occult-ridden peoples to the Way of the Cross, he was to recruit 'Apostles for Christ,' priest if you will, to carry the message throughout the land, the Christian way of faith and morals to live by. He was unsuccessful, having recruited only seven followers in Spain. After much effort, he was depressed and lost at the end of his journey near the end of the earth, at Zaragoza, the most northeastern point in Spain. He, no doubt, being a fisherman by occupation before being Christ's bodyguard, would have caught fish to sustain him. At his lowest point, he made his way to a rock at the cliff's edge and, leaning against it, began a meditative vigil, gazing out to sea.

It was there that Mary, Jesus' Mother, sometime in 40 CE, appeared having arrived in a boat in a vision James later recounted. Mary advised him that his mission had been successful and that he was to build a Church in her honour on that very spot, hand over to the seven of his recruits and return to Jerusalem. He set about creating a stone Church housing a bust-like image of Mary the Mother of his Saviour. The Church caused much interest and controversy among the local fishermen, with whom James won close affinity and was born Christendom in Spain after that.

James returned to Jerusalem soon after completing his mission. The last known record is that Herod Agrippa beheaded him around 44CE (Acts 22:12). Whilst James probably never set foot in Spain in his lifetime, much less ever road a horse and led troops into battle, the myth still stands for his mission. The outcome is still living proof, as the little village now known as Muxia, the favoured endpoint, is beside the fishing village of Finisterre, where the most adventurist pilgrims of The Way choose to end their journey. Muxia is a picturesque fishing town on a small peninsula, well known for its fish and handmade lace. It is best known for the home of Nosa Señora da Barca, "Our Lady of the Boat," and the church built over the rocky shores metres from the crashing wild waves of the ocean there. Apart from the legend of the message of encouragement Mary had given James when she appeared to him, she also gave him an image of herself, which is displayed in the nave to this day. On the second Sunday in September is La Fiesta de Nosa Señora de Barca, 'the Feast day of the lady of the boat.' It is the second most celebrated feast day in the Spanish Catholic church events; the first, of course, is the feast day of St. James at the

Cathedral de Compostela in Santiago. In Muxia, thousands come from far and wide throughout the land to visit the little Church in homage to the Virgin Mary and the beloved St. James. In the village of Muxia, there is a lot of dancing, eating local fish, making a caldera (stew), drinking Spanish wine, and parading the Virgin Mary statue through the street. The only mythological symbol besides the Church at Muxia is the large rock outside where the Virgin Mary's boat remains- 'Pedra da Cadis represents her sail, a kidney-shaped rudder and a rocky stone representing the hull.

Fact or fiction of the stories surrounding the life of St.James in Spain and his apparent journey of The Way has encouraged Pilgrims to walk their own Camino for over a thousand years. My search on The Way had led me from despair to hope, depression to a progressive recovery to health of body, mind and spirit. It is a journey that sowed the seeds of creativity, nestled in a lotus flower within my heart, and still blossoms with poems, stories and songs, some of which are expressed within the pages of this book. I had slain the mythical dragon that had held me captive in my former empire-building years. My quest to build the mansions of material wants and supposed needs had cracked, crumbled and fallen when the supremacy of my inner dragon was brought to rest. So here I will be, on a new pathway advancing towards the kingdom of the wise as every human before their end is a near will, in a moment of regret, wish that they had more time to go live, really live. Humanity, throughout the history of the Universe, has strived to lead, be independent, be at peace, and give and graciously receive as the inner soul would have us believe.

Equally, the things of this world that we strive so earnestly to achieve or to lord over, to hold on to, do ultimately crumble and come to nothing. The motto I have gleaned from my Camino's has taught me to trust only the God of my understandings as all the rest is but a whiff of smoke in the scheme of time, and equally, books I've written are read and soon forgotten. Be that so, it has been cast upon me the duty to keep on writing, to strive for better things for myself and my fellow man, to use my talents to give an account of my stewardship so that future generations may have a reason for living and hoping.

In the beginning, it was the breath of life
that formed the word of God,
expressing the Universal dream
wherein the Earth was formed.

It all began with an explosion,
the Word that was made flesh,
forming planetary motion,
cosmic stars in the Universe.

In the dream was formed
both day and night,
the Sun, the Moon, the stars
many planets and almighty forces,

We understand here on Earth,
Solar System starting nearest the Sun,
working outward, the rocky ones
Mercury, Venus, Earth and Mars.

Then comes the enormous outer,
mostly filled with gas and core,
they are known as the terrestrial planets,
Jupiter, Saturn, Uranus and Neptune, of course.

We could include another one
on a widely titled course,
for it's on a different orbital path,
'planet'(?) Pluto goes it's way.

Then, if you count the 'Planet X,'
right now, it's a mathematical guess,
if and when it passes the planetary test,
including Pluto, which makes ten.

Our Solar System is vast and expansive,
from Earth to the naked eye,
Sun, Moon and majestic stars,
by day and night,
it is wondrous to visualise.

The Earth is home to creatures,
minute, large and small,
and the primarily puzzling one,
it's the human form that us.

God's plan included man,
and like the stars,
we live, we die,
and that's what puzzles us.

CHAPTER 4.

THE SEARCH AND THE FINDING

Everyone has the right to freedom of thought, conscience, and religion. This right includes freedom to change one's religion or belief and freedom, either alone or in community with others and in public or private, to manifest one's religion or belief in worship, teaching, practice, and observance.

"If You are the Christ, tell us." But He told them, "If I tell you, you will not believe;" Luke 22:67. No one can force anyone to believe anything. Each has a choice; it is always ours, whether to accept or not based on the evidence presented. And if there is no evidence that one can discern with logic, then believing is a matter of faith. The absence of evidence does not mean it's not inside you or on the other side of this life. Religious belief can contribute to the community, provide personal support, and offer guidance.

Hermits often sought seclusion to contemplate life and its meaning. Others preferred to be alone because they were more content in that way than in the company of others. They did not need a community or the lifestyle of their fellow man. Likewise, Anchorites were hermits who went to caves or holy places to pursue closer contact with God through meditation and prayer.

"The opium of the people" is a phrase that refers to religion and is derived from a statement by Karl Marx. The full quote is, "Religion is the sigh of the oppressed creature, the heart of a heartless world, and the soul of soulless conditions. It is the opium of the people" Specifically, Marx believed that religion had certain practical functions in society that were similar to the function of opium in a sick or injured person: it reduced people's immediate suffering. It gave them pleasant illusions, giving them strength to carry on.

The religious way of life is different from every other way of life found among humanity. It differs from that of the moral idealist. The idealist picks out of each situation whatever will promote his idea. He ignores, fights or tolerates all the rest. He is blind to all the abundance that overflows or conflicts with his ideal. Then there is the man filled with uninhabited desires and against the idealist stand. His way of living differs from that of the religious, just as much as that of the idealist, but at the opposite extreme. He picks out of the riches of each situation whatever will satisfy his specific desires, but all the rest flows over him unappreciated and inaccessible. The religious man, on the other hand, in contradistinction from both of these, explores sensitively and frequently the emerging new meaning in each situation while holding his desires and ideals in control as experimental instruments to be used in guiding him into situations where they are bound to be transcended or submerged by the richness of value which he cannot possibly apprehend before he experiences it in full concreteness of a consumable acceptable blend.

The steps by which one achieves this way of religious living cannot be taken once and for all. Like an elixir to heal the soul, the religious believer continues to practice the belief repeatedly. He contemplates, prays, and meditates in his isolation. He is a believer, and his religious faith is the life that saves the world. It serves the needs of the individual personality and society in the only ways that enable this age to escape destruction. This spontaneity of free and full religious psychic responsiveness of the prime condition of the human serves as the conditioning for mental health. It has been proven over time that the spiritual way does protect from mental illness. It seems that depression and anxiety inevitability go hand in hand with those who lack belief in God, a religious faith of some sort. Humanity suffers ills when it struggles with the impossible, strives to maintain a particular view of itself in the face of incoming evidence to the contrary, and cannot relinquish some desire in the face of consciences or society that condemns. But all of these disorganising conditions fade out and disappear when the total personality becomes plastic, when it becomes freely and entirely responsible for the best possible outcome in each situation, when it finds the full flood of circumstance, the riches of laughter, or tragedy, and fulfilment but does not cling to the impossible and does not demand that any fixed desire or fixed ideal be satisfied.

To the believer, " religion is life." for religion, wherever it exists. One cannot take it up as one takes up golf by giving it a couple of afternoons a week. That kind of amateur approach is no religion. Religion is either the whole of one's life or no religion. To all these who want religion and want it ' in its place," that is apart from their business, political persuasion, luxuries or conveniences, or anything else is not religion. It is something or other. You had better find its name, but it is not religion. This is why those who seek quiet solitude in prayer and meditation, be they caught up in the material world, doing their best to be in the world but not of it, or as hermit-like individuals retreating in a room, a cave or the quietness of a church, exacting ways that they are called to practice belief, to make conscious contact with the God of their own, asking for guidance to follow the ways of the heart and not the head. Such discipline is a religious practice. It is not easy, but it does help and is a religion to me.

I walked my first Camino de Santiago in the hot summer of June 2013. The temperature never dropped below 42 degrees all day as I tramped The Way of St James, the Apostle of Christ. My daily habit was to cease walking later in the afternoon to find accommodation in the first village I walked through before nightfall.

My tramping The Way was, more often than not, meditation as my feet made continual contact with the earth like the sound of the rhythm of a drum. Upon reaching a village, it was my daily habit to head for the first small church I could find, put down my backpack, and take off my boots to cool my feet. There, I would sit for an extended period of contemplation, taking in the architectural influences of the ancient builders, for each sacred place had historical evidence of the times the Moors ruled Spain, which was equal to that of Christian times. The altars were always ornate, and behind this, dressed in gold leaves symbolic of Spanish influence, stood the tabernacle: The place where the bread and wine are held in a consecrated state, awaiting the communion of the faithful to eat the bread and drink the wine in commemoration of the sacrifice of Christ for humanity and in remembrance of his last supper, where he reportedly said: " Take and eat of this for this is my body, take and drink of this for this is my blood.,do this in memory of me."

Everything in those little churches, such as the Cathedrals of Borgo, Leon, and Santiago, was purpose-built in symbolic reverence. At the entry, a small alcove was traditionally used by the Catechists, those seeking to be accepted into the faith, to stay for the term of learning before they were allowed to enter the church of the faithful congregation. It was also the palace where those who felt unworthy would stay listening to the service of the Mass, a reenactment of the Last Supper. The congregation sat in the pews in the middle of the Church, whilst the altar and tabernacle, symbolic of the Jewish covenant of the lamb's sacrifice to God, are reenacted as Christ, the sacrificial lamb of God. Everything within the building is traditionally symbolic of this event. The congregation is called the body of the people, and when they receive communion, the priest says: " The Body of Christ.' those who accept the host and the wine, in turn, respond. " Amen" means: " So may it be."

I have been reflecting on the symbols and signs within the little churches. The pews where the congregation is seated are called the body of the church, whilst to the left of the altar is the Epistle side where the bulletins and correspondence are stored as was traditional. On the right side is the Gospel, where the priest changes into vestments to celebrate the Mass. The Altar and tabernacle represent where Christ's consecrated hosts reside. So, the entry to the Church is like the lower regions of the body; the middle of the Church, where the congregation resides, is the Body, and the Epistle and Gospel sides are symbolic of the two arms of Christ. The head is where the altar and tabernacle can be viewed. A thought comes to my mind that

Christ controls the body of the people, for the body cannot rule the head. The head always leads and controls the body,

My retreating to the church gave me pause to contemplate the meaning of faith. The crucifix of Christ's final hour as He appears on a cross, Mary the Mother of Jesus statues depicting her holding the child Jesus, the saints representative of leading a sacrificial life, the stations of the cross around the walls depicting Christ tramping his way to calvary, and the whole building itself. It surprises me now that I gave up that faith. It was the symbols and signs from my childhood faith that I miss most in my Catholic education, but regrettably, I've moved on, perhaps unwisely, as I look back in hindsight.

One of the most common ways to fit life into rigid definitions is to qualify something, whether a person, a thing, or an idea, with the statement, "This belongs to me." However, because life is this elusive and perpetually changing process, every time we think we have taken possession of something, we have completely lost it. All that we possess is our idea about the thing desired, an idea that tends to remain fixed and does not grow as the thing grows. Thus, one of the most noticeable facts about those obsessed with greed for possessions, whether they be goods or cherished ideas, is their desire that things will remain as they are- not only that their possessions shall stay in their hand, but also the possessions themselves shall not change. Some theologians and philosophers show the most significant concern if anyone questions their idea about the universe, for they imagine that within those ideas, they have ultimately enshrined the ultimate truth and that to lose those ideas would be to lose the truth. As truth is alive, it can not be bound by anything that shows no signs of life—namely, a conception whose validity depends partly on the fact that it is unchangeable. For once we imagine we have grasped the truth of life, the truth has vanished, for truth cannot become anyone's property, the reason being that truth is life, and for one person to think that he possesses all life is a manifest absurdity. Just as no person can define it, for the idea of possession is illusory.

Spiritual freedom is a capacity to be spontaneous and unfettered as life itself, as the wind that blows, where it swirls and the sound it makes when it comes; we cannot tell from where it comes nor where it is going. "Even so, "said Jesus," everyone born is born of The Spirit." But non-attachment does not mean running away from things to some peaceful hermitage, for we can never escape from our illusions about life; we carry them with us, and if we are afraid of them and wish to escape, it means we are doubly enslaved. Whether content with illusions or frightened of them, they possess us equally. Hence, the non-attachment of Buddhism and Thaoism means not running away from life but running with it, for freedom comes through complete acceptance of reality. Those who wish to keep their illusions do not move; those who fear them run backwards into even more incredible illusions, while those who conquer them 'walk on.'

For the life of a hermit, a wanderer, a pilgrim of the road is a movement of the Spirit, of the emptiness of transitory things; nothing can be grasped, for everything is empty. In the vast nothingness, it is no-thing-ness…the void… it is in a meditative state where God exists. We do not move to be in a rut; we exist in the freedom of the Spirit. The very nature of the state cannot be described in words. To draw an analogy, it.is like the wind moving across the earth, never stopping at any particular place, never attaching itself to any specific object or another, constantly adapting itself to the rise and fall of the ground.

If such an analogy gives the impression of a dreamy, laissez-faire attitude to life, it must be remembered that this Zen-like state is not always a gentle breeze. More often than not, it is a fierce gale that sweeps everything ruthlessly before it, an icy blast that penetrates the heart of everything and passes right through to the other side! As I previously stated, those who fall into this area of finding freedom and poverty leave everything and " walk on," for they realise this is what life itself does; it is the religion of life!

So it is that the masters of such discipline are the disciples of a belief that came to them long before they came to practice the art of getting in the zone of the Spirit self. It is tragic how few people ever " possess their souls" before they die. " nothing is rare in any Man, "Says Ralph Waldo Emerson.." than an act of his own." It is pretty accurate; most people are other people."Their thoughts are someone else opinion, and their lives mimic others' passion and quotations. We all fall for this somewhat, particularly those who write books and research information. My duty is not to depend too much on other ideas but to create my own based on my understanding and act accordingly in my everyday life.

When Christ says," Forgive your enemies," it is not for the sake of the enemy but for one's own sake that he says so, and it is because love is more beautiful than hate. In his bidding to the young man, " Sell all that thou hast, and give it to the poor," it is not the state of the poor that he is thinking, but the soul of the young man, the soul that wealth was marring…While Christ did not say to me, "Live for others," he pointed out that there were no differences between the lives of others and one's own life. By this means, he gave the man an extended personality of strength and intellect.

CHAPTER 5.

PROGRESSION OF THE WAY

One must be able to strip oneself of all self-deception, to see oneself naked in one's own eyes before one can come to terms with the elements of oneself and know who one is. That is why the life of a hermit has its place at some point in one's life.

A traveller on a new path of destiny may well discover the Reality of living in the present. New horizons may open up. Be it an artist's talent, that of a musician or a man of Science that emerges, it may well bring with it some new level of being in the moment, handing over to a power greater than self, or in so doing, an enduring period of much suffering may have to be endured with disciplined self-denial or a learning curve that takes one from the depth of despair to a new joyful plain of existence. It may form the light or the darkness. Often, the creative self emerges after a long period of the night of the soul. The recipient may find that it becomes as much a curse as a blessing in disguise. Ultimately, the application for the newfound talent dies down, and the creative self begins to work not for their benefit but for our fellowman.

It is sometimes difficult to get into the practice of living in accord with the Spirit. Mediocrity then becomes the rule. It is easy to see how the religious Way, particularly the way of a hermit, can cease to hold out an answer to man's longing for fulfilment and fall into disrepute. We may wonder why advice concerning progression has been made available. The lack of information in this area and enlightened instruction of early religious direction has long been available and frequently neglected. A body of information supplied by psychology sheds light on the unconscious factors involved in any character change. Also, there has come an increasing influx of translations from a wealth of ancient Hindu and Buddhist sources concerning how man can learn to apprehend Reality. We of Western belief can profit from some of the methods these religions have developed, even though some of the techniques these religions have do not fit the mould of our Western temperament.

The following information and advice have been gleaned from these areas of insight and contemporary religious teachers.

Space limitation prevents a thorough consideration of all known concerning progression on the Way. You, the reader, may profit by further study concerning them. Consider Psychological Types by Carl G. Jung and Varieties of Temperament by William R Shelton, for starters. The factors governing the rate and range are complex and individually determined. Biological heritage, mental and emotional endowment, temperament, and environmental factors enter. Recent psychological studies on physical and temperamental types are helpful in spiritual training.

We often need to remind ourselves that every step offers immeasurable benefits. Therefore, we must use every sound means to accelerate our progress, knowing that the final range of achievement depends not on our efforts but on God's grace.

In the words of Lao-tzu, Chinese philosopher, 6th century BC: "A tree that takes both arns to encircle grew from a tiny rootlet. A many-storied pagoda is built by placing one brick upon another brick. A journey of three thousand miles begins with a single step."

In the great mystics, we see the highest and most comprehensive development of that consciousness that the human race has yet to attain. We see its growth exhibited to us on a grand scale, based on perceptions by humanity. The germ of the same transcendent life, the spring of the fantastic energy that enables the great mystic to rise to freedom and dominate his world, is latent in all of us, an integral part of our humanity.

Nowhere do mystics have a genius for the absolute; we each have a little of his talent, some greater, some less. Once we permit its emergence, the growth of this talent, this soul spark, will conform in miniature and, according to its measure, to those laws of organic growth, those inexorable conditions of transcendence that are found to govern the Mystic Way.

Every person who awakens to consciousness of a reality that transcends the everyday world of sense is put upon a road that follows low levels, the path that the mystic treads at a higher level. It matters little if you are an artist or a musician trying to capture some aspect of the heavenly light or music while denying all other elements of the world.

We all must realise that when we go astray in our attitudes towards ourselves, we become enslaved to false notions of what we are and ought to be. Some of us think we love ourselves when we are strangling or suffocating ourselves with morbid self-concern. When we free ourselves from false self-love, which is narcissism, we can become unconscious victims of our paralysed egocentricities.

We must become wise enough to realise where we go astray in our attitude towards ourselves and how we become enslaved to false notions of what we are and ought to be. Some of us think we love ourselves when we are strangling or suffocating ourselves with morbid self-concern. We maintain a cruel contempt for our capability and witness or become friendly with ourselves and others. When we take time out to relax, meditate, pray or find a place of solitude like a hermit, we are on the road to self-love.No man or woman can have self-respect unless he/she has learned the art of renunciation and equally, the vital art of self-acceptance. Such self-love implies many things, but it is rooted in self-respect.

In my former life, I lived with an alcoholic state of mind. It applied not only to my excessive compulsive drinking but to my frantic workaholism, the workload I burdened myself with and the pace at which I lived to make it in this world. I subconsciously sort applause that I now realise had more to do with my childhood abandonment than the need for praise and applause. I've had fame and fortune, but both ultimately slipped away. Though I tried to make it again with excessive striving, time and the reality of its fleeting feelings soon faded. Now, in my dotage, I realise how futile it all was in the chasing, like trying to catch the wind while having it against me. It has taken a lifetime and the last two decades of sobriety to learn, set my boat of personality upon the spiritual waters of life, trim the sail, and go with the flow. All it takes, a day at a time, is an occasional touch of the rudder with prayer and meditation, so to speak, to stay on course.

I'm now conscious of my mistakes in my former lack of integrity, for it is not honest for me to seek prestige. Even though I have a large following of people on social media and market my books through the likes of Amazon, Barnes and Noble, and Walmart, to name but a few, the songs I've written are highlighted daily on music links like Spotify am conscious of the dangers of self-promotion, for it has a subconscious effect on the inner spiritual journey. I still find it challenging to learn the lesson of living in this world and not being a part of it. That is why there is a great deal of peace and serenity in the lifestyle of Anchorites and hermits.

I know that publicity has no place in the Alcoholics Anonymous programme and the miracle it has produced in my friends of the fellowship and me; in avoiding applause and the rewards of world fame, I am a better man for it all. As the author of many books and songs, it has taken me time to step aside and recognise that I am just a conduit for creative output for the benefit of others, be it a mental, spiritual, or monetary reward.

Whilst publicity and self-promotion are hazards to my spiritual progress, I will continue to write, publish, and promote for the foreseeable future. However, my work effort is more like selling a brand than Doug's. My legacy has been created, and I need not do more for fear of being forgotten. All men are ultimately ignored, even by their loved ones, as they go about their busy day of making a living to care for their offspring. I take comfort in the fact that my grandchildren or great-grandchildren may find comfort and insight from my legacy in living their lives after I've long since left the planet.

Whilst my decade of adventures in the northern and southern hemispheres taught me much about self-survival, getting in tune with the creativity that resulted in the outpouring of many books and songs has taken many lessons in selflessness and letting go of egocentricity, in coming to realise other forces in my unconscious are for my betterment that of others which has little to do with my stories and songs. It took a descent into hell before I came out the other side with a conscious attitude to fight fear face to face, and it has been with the guidance of the AA steps programme that I began moving along a different pathway in life.

While I am still caught up in the material world, I am now more mindful daily of the short time this plan has been hatched with divine guidance for me. I believe I am at the cusp of moving on to the inner joy that awaits me in God's plan, which has always been ordained for me. All men come to this, and many can't take it. It is only by being patient, letting go, and listening to the inner guidance that his ultimate plan is revealed.

If you examine the relationship between God and your soul, you will find certain limits to which you refuse to offer yourself to Him. Humanity often hides such reservations, believing not to see them for fear of self-reproach, guarding them as the apple of the eye.

Most men have dual impressions of themselves, two pictures of their selves in isolation from each other. All the portraits of their virtues hung in one room, done in bright, splashing, glorious colours but with no shadows and no balance. In the other room hangs all self-condemnation.

Instead of isolating these two pictures, we must look at them together and gradually blend them. In our exalted moods, we are afraid to admit our personality's guilty, hateful, and shameful elements. In our depressed moods, we are scared to credit ourselves with the goodness and achievements that are ours.

We must begin to draw a new portrait and accept and know ourselves for who we are. We are relative, not absolute, creatures; everything we do is imperfect. So often, people foolishly try to become rivals of God and make demands of themselves that only God could make of Himself—rigid demands of absolute perfection…

A splendid freedom awaits us when we realise that we need not feel like mortal lepers or emotional outcasts because we have some aggressive, hostile thoughts and feelings toward ourselves or others. When we act with these feelings, we no longer have to pretend to be what we are not. We discover that rigid pride is the supreme foe of inner victory. Flexible humility, the kind of humility that applies when we do not demand the impossible or the angelic of ourselves, is the great ally of psychic peace.

We should learn to rejoice in the truth that human beings consist of various moods, impulses, traits, and emotions…

If we become pluralistic in our thinking about ourselves, we shall learn to accept the depressed, cruel, or uncooperative mood for what it is—one of many fleeting, not permanent, states of mind. As acclamation, we accept ourselves for better or worse; we cease demanding a brittle perfection that can lead only to inner despair. Every person's makeup has facets of failure, as there are elements of success. Both must be accepted while we try to emphasise the latter through self-knowledge.

In AA's Step 4, we are encouraged to search fearlessly and carry out a moral inventory of ourselves. We want to discover how our behaviours have caused unhappiness for others and ourselves. In Step 5, we sought to share our character defects with another to help find guidance for our shortcomings, and in Step 6, we asked God for guidance to remove our character defects, which is a tall order. I am reminded of St. Paul's statement in Romans 7: 15-20

"I do not understand what I do. For what I want to do, I do not do, but what I want, I do. And if I do what I do not want, I agree that the law is good. As it is, it is no longer me who does it, but it is a sin living in me. For I know that by my human nature, God itself does not dwell in me, that is, in my sinful nature. I desire to do what is good, but I cannot do it. I do not do the good I want to do, but the evil I do not want to do—this I keep doing. Now, if I do what I do not want to, it is no longer me who does it; it is sin living in me who does it. For what I do out of love I do for you (God)" So it is that I come to believe that my defects of character are slow to be removed as it is I who gets in the way of God's plan for me. So, I must learn to trust in the slow work of God in this regard, but I believe that I will never be utterly free of my sinful nature as it is like man to be. So it is that recognising this, I must meditate and pray on his plan for me irrespective of my defects of character.

In Step 8, we made a list of all the persons we had harmed and became willing to make amends for them. Mindful in Step 9 that we were willing to make direct amends to those we offended wherever possible, except when to do so would injure them or others. Thus, we continued (Step 10) to take a daily personal inventory, and when we were wrong, we promptly admitted it. My concept of a higher power has become the basis for writing books, many of which are spiritually centred on the steps of AA.

"Sought through prayer and meditation to improve our conscious contact with God as we understood Him, praying only for knowledge of His will for us and the power to carry that out."In this 11th step of AA, improving our conscious contact with God reflects our spiritual path and is our ultimate goal. Step Eleven is the daily practice and experience of deepening our awareness of one's belief in a Higher Power through prayer and meditation. You can pray and meditate, regardless of your background or history. If you set aside the time daily, you can reach for whatever you believe is more significant than, more profound than, or beyond yourself. Step Eleven also assumes that by now, you have a conscious awareness of your Higher Power and are drawn to deepening that connection.

The purge of our selfish nature and the dissolving defects is best achieved through Godly worship via meditation and prayer. Reflective meditation, holding specific ideas in mind, focusing on a mantra, or just listening to the breath enables emotional connection, breaking up the crust of old habits to create a new will. Equally, prayer is the most perfect of divine actions to attune ourselves to God's thoughts, which may become an indispensable necessity. Finding that space to be of one mind in prayer is the disciplined opening to the self to God.

Spiritual meditation is an experience that takes you to the depths of who you are. As your authentic self, you are stripped of all your perceptions about yourself until that point in your life. In the process, you experience a feeling of love and light warming up your being. The trouble is, in our fast-paced world, we need to meditate more. The hermit's journey emphasises the importance of meditation for spiritual growth and personal well-being. Meditation is vital for connecting with one's inner self and God. It is described as a journey of self-discovery, inner transformation, and spiritual awareness. Through meditation, individuals can access the love and light of the Divine, which helps to remove the layers of illusion that obscure the soul. The hermit's journey suggests that in today's fast-paced world, there is a need for increased meditation. The Hermits way further highlights the benefits of meditation by drawing parallels with the lives of hermits and the practice of silence. Hermits, who often lived in solitude, used meditation to contemplate life's meaning and connect with God. Engaging in silence and stripping away external distractions are presented as essential steps in achieving a deeper connection with the eternal presence.

The hermit's journey implies that meditation helps individuals gain perspective on their lives, diminish the impact of their worries and anxieties, and strengthen their resolve. Furthermore, the sources suggest that meditation facilitates spiritual growth and the application of spiritual principles in daily life. Meditation is described as a way to make faith more vivid and realise religious beliefs practically. It is recommended as a tool for reflecting on and implementing God's word and guidance.

CHAPTER 6.

MEDITATION & PRAYER

The road back from the brink was full of fear, shame and heartbreak. I had been down a well of depression, loss of confidence in God, and the cravings of one addicted to the need for a drink to drown away my sad, painful life. In time, I slowly began to recover with the help of medical professional advice, the guidance of the AA fellowship, prayer and meditation, and a new enthusiasm to be freed by the spirit of adventure.

I had moved into a small unit near a secluded beach on the Mid-North Coast of New South Wales. It was adequate for my needs, with kitchen space, a small lounge, a ground-floor eat-out area, a washing machine and dryer in a garage, and two bedrooms. One I used for storage, the other I slept in. The night was a drug-induced sleep from a sleeping pill. Then came the daylight hours of a depressed state of mind. I had determined not to let the night of the soul engulf me.

My day began and ended with silent action. I always jumped out of bed before I had time to think, dressed in shorts, a T-shirt, socks, and joggers, and made my way to the beach, a ten-minute walk from where I existed. I walked a kilometre through midtown and onto the beach for a three-kilometre walk up and back. I returned to my humble abode for 30 minutes of meditation and a breakfast of juice, cereal, yoghurt, and berries. Then, without further ado, I packed a backpack with apple, baked beans, a spoon, mixed nuts, and adequate water to see me through the day and headed out again for a bush trail walk or mountain trail venture. Apart from stopping to eat something or take a drink, I would walk all day or lay down in the bush beside a tree and ask God to take away my suffering. He never did in those six months of living like a hermit, but he did in his own good time.

For the next five years, I attended and experimented with every meditative practice known to man. Ultimately, I settled on daily reflective readings, breathing meditation, and yoga exercises. Even though I started practising yoga twelve years ago, I still do those practices most days.

[If faith is to be made vivid, it must be done through meditation. We are told that" Faith cometh by hearing." But we have to do more than merely listen to it. Meditation is meant to make our Faith real to us so that we shall realise what we know and believe in our lives.] Spiritual Letters by Dom John Chapman.

Spiritual meditation is a profound practice that allows us to connect with the inner self-link with God; by redirecting our attention from the outer world, during meditation, we focus on the inner gateway to this inner garden, and we can embark on a journey to experience the love and Light of God. This connection with the Divine's love removes layers of mind, matter, and illusion that shroud our soul. Higher self and tap into the wisdom and guidance within us. It is a journey of self-discovery, inner transformation, and deepening spiritual awareness.

I was thinking as the hermit now, and I spoke to myself as I journaled these words: [Let any true man go into silence, strip himself of all pretence, selfishness, sensuality, and sluggishness of soul; lift off thought after thought, passion after passion, till he reaches the innermost depth of all; remember how short a time and how he was not at all; how short a time again, and he will not be here, open his window and look upon the night, how still its breath, how solemn its march, how deep its perspective, how ancient form of light; and think how little he knows except the infinity of God and the mysteriousness of life:-and it will be strange if he does not feel the Eternal Presence as close upon his soul as the breeze upon his brow; if he does not say, " O Lord, art thou ever near as this, and have I not known that?"

Suppose the proper proportions and the genuine spirit of life do not open on his heart with infinite clearness and show him the littleness of his temptations and the grandeur of his trust. He is ashamed to have found weariness in toil so light and tears where there was no trial to the brave. He discovers with astonishment how small the dust has blinded him, and from the height of quiet and holy love, he looks down with incredulous sorrow on the jealousies, fears, and irritations that have vexed his life. A mighty wind of resolution sets in strong upon him and freshens the whole atmosphere of his soul, sweeping down before it the light flakes of difficulty till they vanish like snow upon the sea. He is imprisoned more in a small compartment of time but belongs to an eternity, which is now and here. The isolation of his separate spirit passes away, and with the countless souls akin to God, he is but a wave of his unbounded deep. He is at one with Heaven and has found the Almighty's secret place.]

I was thinking about all my efforts in writing books and recording my songs and how I go to great lengths to prompt them to the world. I so often say to my fellows who are still suffering alcoholics that we are square pegs trying to fit into round holes. In our sobriety in the fellowship of Alcoholics Anonymous, we come to realise and believe that we are destined to live by the spirit of God. We may live in this world but not be living 'of' the world.

Accordingly, Mark 8:36 exhorts believers to reflect on their life choices and prioritise their devotion to Christ. It suggests that the accurate measure of success lies not in worldly wealth but in faithfulness and spiritual integrity. The ultimate question remains: What will we exchange for our souls?

Carl Jung's most famous idea is his quote, "We ought not to live the afternoon of our lives as we lived the morning of our lives." He recognised the psychological value of spiritual experience, particularly when traditional religious belief was waning and church attendance was declining. It could be construed that he was also relating to the fact that in our dotage, we need to let go of the things of this world to focus on our spiritual essence and service to God and our fellow man.

[One person who has mastered life is better than a thousand persons who have mastered the contents of books, for no one can get anything out of life without God. If I were looking for a master's degree, I would have to go to Paris to the colleges where higher studies are pursued, but if I wanted to know more about the perfection of life, they could not tell me there. Here, then, should I go? to someone with a pure and gentle nature free of all pretence, worldly desires, and nowhere else? Therefore, I should find the answer to my anxious inquiry.] Meister Johannes Eckhart, German scholar and mystic.

We cannot know our inner world directly as we know our heartbeat or pulse. The actions and reactions of our primitive mental image inherited from our earliest human ancestors are supposed to be in our DNA, present in our collective unconscious through symbols. We know these images through our conditioning, stories told to us, or what we have deduced from within; we know these images stand for something other than themselves. Symbols always have vistas of mystery standing behind them. If they do not, they are signs, as traffic signals and not as a symbol.

Our symbols shall know us. Symbols carry and express our uniqueness and ordinariness. They make life as bright or dark imaginations. The artist cannot live without symbols and is sometimes highly aware of them. The child lives unconsciously and spontaneously through them....

Most adults live without being aware symbols constantly surround them, and in themselves, their existence is lacklustre and meaningless. If the earth could speak, it might say: "How can I tell the man I am here to serve and be served by him?" And if the unconscious world of man speaks, it might utter: "I, too, am here to serve and be served." I will tell him through buds and blossoms in spring, whole fruit in harvest, and winter silence." "I will tell him through symbols woven into dreams, myths, religious rituals, art, the play of children, and into all persons or situations or things which move him with joy, grief, fear, anger, diaspora and love."

As soon s he looks into the mirror of the waters we are faced to the diversity of our being, best to worst, by way of symbols. And if the "all" is to be used toward wholeness of living and loving, religiously meaningful life needs to be based on symbols of life made conscious.

I got to thinking about my role in serving and being served and, in the process, how best I fit into this world, but not being of it, and yet continue to write my books and promote them for the greater good. In keeping with my understanding of my need to maintain a confident presence in the marketplace and yet maintain my state, I must be mindful of what I lose as a consequence of either action and what is to be gained therein.

Anonymity describes situations in which the acting person's identity is unknown. Some writers have argued that namelessness, though technically correct, does not capture what is more centrally at stake in anonymity contexts. The critical idea is that a person must be non-identifiable, unreachable, or untraceable. Anonymity is seen as a technique or a way of realising specific values, such as privacy or liberty.

In Alcoholics Anonymous, and at the personal level, anonymity protects all members from identification as alcoholics, a safeguard often of particular importance to newcomers. At the press, radio, TV, and film level, anonymity stresses the equality in the Fellowship of all members by breaking those who might otherwise exploit their A.A. affiliation to achieve recognition, power, or personal gain.

How much anonymity is necessary for an alcoholic like me to maintain the AA traditions and still promote my works for the world to see? Well, it must be said that it is more critical to protect the anonymity of my fellow alcoholics for identification as alcoholics, a safeguard often of particular importance to newcomers. Understanding anonymity states: "Our public relations policy is based on attraction rather than promotion; we need always maintain personal anonymity at the level of press, radio, and films."

A newcomer may want to tell others about his newfound pathway to freedom in the AA Steps programme to recovery. He may turn to those who have helped him, like his medical practitioner, religious adviser, close friend, or family member. With renewed confidence, he may also tell his employer and business associates. So when the opposition to unity as helpful came along, he could talk about AA to almost anyone.

These quiet disclosures helped him to lose his fear of the alcoholic stigma and spread the news of A. AA.'s existence in his community. Many new men and women came to AA because of such conversations. Since it is only at the top public level that anonymity is essential, such communication was well with its spirit.

Whilst I use social media and other promotional channels to market my books and songs, it is not so much to promote myself personally but as a brand, as with my books, to gain sales. However, there is a risk of overstepping the mark from my perspective and giving the wrong impression to newcomers to the AA programme. I am employing to have others promote my work instead of being too foxy by myself on the outcomes. There is always an Achilles heel to my argument, so I have to maintain a specific distance from what I do in this regard and be mindful that my anonymity has its place within AA and outside the program. It applies to others. I tread a fine line In this process.

Looking back over this time, I can see clearly that the Twelve Steps have become God's surprising way of keeping my life on track. I have little doubt that without their wisdom and practical guidance, my life would have been much poorer today at every level. They have given me a way of dealing with my tendency toward compulsive behaviour, helped me take a closer look at my weaknesses and provided me with practical tools for spiritual growth and healing. In a nutshell, the Twelve Steps have become profoundly helpful in my ongoing journey of change.

Sometimes, a story can be a powerful way to learn and grow. No wonder recovery centres on telling our story and emphasising our "experience, strength, and hope."

The central block to my progress in AA is Step 3, which involves not so much accepting God's will as my guiding influence in living a spiritual life as handing my will and my life over to Him and applying what He has planned for me.

When it comes to God's word, my problem is not reading it, memorising it, learning it, or even knowing it; my problem is implementing his plan. I can have the knowledge of God in the Twelve Steps, but only when it is applied will it bring Him honour. You can train a parrot to repeat the steps of AA, but it will never change the parrot. Some people live their entire lives without really building upon the proper foundation. When the floods come, their spiritual structures crumble because they only hear and never heed. The actual test of our spiritual character is not how we receive the message of The Steps but how we appropriate it in our lives. But how do we do it? How do we take what we have read from the Steps and carry the message?

Reading and meditating alone will not bring application, but you have to start somewhere. If you need to read the Steps, how can you apply them? How can you abide by the Steps of AA if you don't know them? If you don't know the various pieces of the armour of God, how can you wear them? The spiritual application of God's guidance begins inwardly – get the message in your heart first, and then watch it unfold throughout everyday living.

As you meditate on the Words in the Steps, ask the Lord to give you understanding and discernment. Pray over the text and ask God for spiritual enlightenment. Reflect on the text throughout the day. Seek clarity, insight, and instruction, and believe God will impart such knowledge (James 1:5).

What is God saying to me? How do I apply the Steps in my life? Ask specifically how a particular principle pertains to your life. Begin measuring your habits, decisions, and attitudes with Steps, then adjust accordingly. Seek the help of longer-standing members in the fellowship of Alcoholics Anonymous.

I also have to look to the bible from time to time. Filter each situation through the Word of God, and make decisions according to Scripture. Allow me to give you one example – let's look at Ephesians 4:29, "Let no corrupt communication proceed out of your mouth, but that which is good to the use of edifying, that it may minister grace unto the hearers." This verse teaches us to monitor our conversations. Not only should we refrain from gossip, but we should also use our discussions to enlighten others. The next time you engage in conversation, keep this verse in your mind and your mouth. In every situation, there is an opportunity to implement Bible truth.

It is a sword that pierces to the deepest asunder of the soul. When we prepare to make a biblical application, we must prepare our hearts for change. We do not change God's Word; His Word changes us...and always for our benefit and advantage. Allow God's Word to speak to you and then through you. It is an affinity that applies to the steps of AA in my life application.

CHAPTER 7.

HERMIT'S PEACEFUL PLACE

I am sitting in my home office, making out like a hermit as I write these lines. I live in a modern society where I am provided with the tools to be a hermit like no other. As I choose, I can earn a living from behind a computer screen, pay my bills online, and order food to be delivered. Anything I want can be ordered and dropped off without interacting with another person. At what other time in history was this possible?

Our ancestors had to leave society to be hermits. They could not exist in the middle of society as hermits, but currently, we have the technology and social structure to be digital hermits. Can a person easily live in the middle of an urban jungle without interacting with another human for weeks, months, or years?

People often become hermits **to** protest society's ills, find God, find themselves, pursue the arts, or eliminate everyday stress. The hermit mindset values people over things. As family generations retreat to their 'cave', the main treasure to cherish is conversation with people. I choose to isolate myself when I am in the process of pursuing a creative pursuit, such as writing this novel. In the past, I retreated into isolation to deal with depression and anxiety as a consequence of my world turning upside down. It was at a time when I was flying high with the material world of success, striving for more and never satisfied until I could relax at the end of the day with a drink to soothe the savage beast that lay within.

When all that I knew and seemingly possessed turned to dust, I retreated to a modern-day cave near a beach and bushland to lick my wounded pride and begin my recovery process. I was protecting myself against the world's ravages and finding some way out towards enlightenment. I did not know it then, but it would come spiritually, and I would develop an understanding of myself while walking the Camino de Santiago. It was a lesson in learning to let go of the ego to embrace myself in a pilgrim's journey.

So, on my outward journey on the Camino, I emerged from darkness into the light of day with a lotus flower of creative ideas. I return to my cave-like existence at home to nurture the innovative ideas that emerged into prolific writing and music creation periods. To maintain balance with the world at large in my new realisation that I was to live in the world but not of the world, I began to attend regular meetings of Alcoholics Anonymous, installing the Steps of the program into my daily routine. So, in my solitude, I had the space for introspection, self-reflection, meditation, and prayer. The inward journey is not always easy, and the creative output I never knew was my way out of my former period of hardship and suffering.

Living in the world but not of the world does not mean that we have to give up our material wants and needs; it is just that they do not play such an essential part in our lives as we put the ego in its place, a little ego is not such a bad thing just as long as we allow it to be just like a grain of sand upon a beach and keeping it in check so it doesn't take over as the whole beach so to speak. It is not about living a hermit-like existence to escape the world but more about transforming our relationship with the world, finding inner peace and understanding to return to the world with a renewed sense of purpose for others and a desire to serve others.

The hermit's journey unveils one's true self, shedding layers of conditioning and social expectations to reveal the authentic individual within. This process is often accompanied by the emergence of creativity and a deeper connection to nature. The hermit journey is a testament to the transformative power of self-discovery. The hermit finds meaning, purpose, and a profound sense of peace by embracing solitude and seeking a deeper connection with the inner self and a higher power.

I returned to the Camino thrice for further healing and renewal of creativity that emerged due to my journeys. It is important to note that the sources presented this hermit's journey as a personal and unique experience. Each individual has a unique path, and their journey may not necessarily be as a pilgrim on the Camino de Santiago with enlightened creativity. It is fair to say that whatever pathway one takes may be a Camino experience. There is no single prescribed path, and it will unfold according to one's unique circumstances and spiritual understanding.

In my case, it was a series of events that culminated in my hermit-like retreat, a period of great introspection and spiritual seeking, for I had lost connection with the God I traditionally accepted as my guiding light. In truth, I was in a dark place and could not see any light or way out of my circumstances. The events of personal loss, internal struggle, and a yearning for deeper meaning formed the foundation of the transformative journey that has since emerged. Losing family and fortune was one thing, but the upheaval in a spate of depression and despair pushed me to solace and answers beyond the material world.

I was disillusioned with worldly pursuits but somehow had to go through another cycle of trying to regain what I had lost: power, money and prestige. I was that square peg trying to fit into a round hole that I have mentioned elsewhere in this story. Each hardship that followed chipped away at the marble of my former heart desires until I met a manifest belief of a Christ-like figure on the Way who has led me to the direction I now travel. The guiding light I cannot describe is trust that I am on the right path with fitness and freedom I've never known.

The hermit's journey is only sometimes clearcut. He must acknowledge that it is an ongoing process of growth and refinement, of acknowledging imperfections, and of embracing the multifaceted nature of the human experience. The reality of accepting the positive and negative aspects of oneself and striving for progress rather than absolute perfection.

I am attempting to portray the hermit's journey within the deeper self, seeking more profound meaning and purpose beyond the material world as we know it. Solitude is the first step to self-sufficiency and creative expression, which provides insight into the challenges and rewards of a path to follow in modern society. There is a paradox: we must remain engaged with the world while detached from material pursuits. It is treading the pathway of life and being as vigilant as female serpents in ensuring that the ego does not overrule our spiritual goals. We must remain acutely conscious, awake to the present moment, and responsive to a newfound purpose, which may manifest in various forms, such as artistic expression, acts of service, or a commitment to living a more spiritually aligned life. The pilgrim's journey is not simply about enduring physical challenges; it's about embracing the transformative power of those challenges, too.

While it may be construed that the hermit might be "running away" from reality, the sources, particularly the authors' account, present a more subtle perspective. It's not a simple case of escapism but rather a deliberate choice to engage with reality differently, prioritising introspection, spiritual growth, and service over material pursuits and societal expectations.

I challenge the notion of "manning up" as conforming to a conventional definition of engagement with the modern world. My experiences suggest that true strength lies in confronting inner demons to seek a deeper understanding of oneself. This often involves a retreat and introspection, not as an escape from reality but as a means to better align with more authentic surroundings and better understand ourselves and our place in this world. The journey is not about physical isolation but deliberate cultivation of inner peace and spiritual awareness, ultimately leading to a deeper understanding of oneself and one's place in the universe.

I acknowledge that the distinction between hermits and anchorites can be blurry, especially in a contemporary context. My journey, in which I sought a spiritual life like an anchorite, engaging in religious practices in churches and sacred sites, evolved beyond the structure framework to a journey of human connection, even amidst a trip focused on solitude. My poetry served as a validation and encouragement, unlocking a creative potential that might have remained dormant. This encounter underscores the unexpected ways inspiration can emerge and profoundly impact seemingly insignificant moments that shape an individual's life path.

In recognition of my earlier life of disconnect between my true nature and the expectations I had of the world, it was through childhood memories that I had found true freedom in nature, not that of the material world; I recall the advice i received after my initial breakdown which I have previous referred to in this book:

" Put your boat of personality upon the spiritual waters of life and go with the flow."

The Camino de Santiago played a crucial role in shaping my creative journey. It inspired and facilitated a pivotal encounter that unlocked the potential of my songwriting and novel and was a rich source of metaphors for spiritual explorations. The Camino's impact is evident in my creative output's volume and thematic focus, solidifying its place as a transformative force in my life and work.

I indeed emerged from my encounter with inner darkness transformed. What I initially perceived as a ' dragon's mouth' revealed itself to be a 'lotus flower of creative ideas.' This powerful imagery reflects the transformative power of the Camino, suggesting that facing my inner demons emerges as a more straightforward way of coming to terms with myself through writing books and songs.

My first Camino experience was a multifaceted journey of healing, self-discovery, and creative awakening. It was a pilgrimage driven by a need to confront past pain, surrender to the present moment, and embrace the unknown. This experience highlights Camino's transformative potential, demonstrating the capacity to facilitate profound inner peace and harmony without being dazzled by what the world offers as an alternative.

This pilgrimage of life suggests that the hermit's journey is not solely about personal enlightenment but also about contributing to the well-being of others. Whilst anonymity along the lines of Alcoholics Anonymous Steps and Traditions plays a vital role, I am torn between the desire to share my creative works and the ongoing negotiation between the inward focus of the hermit's path and the outward expression of the world and service to others. There is a grappling tension between the hermit's desire for solitude and the inherent human need for connection and contribution. In drawing upon my experience in the confines of Alcoholics Anonymous, anonymity is a core principle. To explore the challenge of balancing personal privacy with the desire to share one's story with the world, I acknowledge the importance of the anonymity of others while recognising the potential benefits of using my experiences and creative output to inspire and support those in need.

Finding the balance requires careful discernment. I emphasise the need for the hermit's service to be offered with humility, avoiding self-promotion, and prioritising the well-being of others. I also emphasise the importance of introspection, meditation, creative expression, and service to find meaning, purpose, and connection on a spiritual path that embraces solitude and engagement with the world.

Sinking stone.

Cast a stone into water,
watched the wake trails fade,
life is like that, a fading thing,
watching the ripples,
as they lap upon the shore.

Cast my burden like a stone,
into the river of life...
watched the ripples as
they fade away upon the shore.

Feel the wind ripple the water,
like loves and dreams of the past,
the wake trails of water to shore,
It all just fades, and it dies.

Put down the book and the pencil,
leave the old guitar aside,
let go of the songs of the memories,
It's all wake trails to the shore.

Just fading memories of the past,
they do not last for long,
like wake trails to the water,
like wake trails to the shore.

Wanderer on the Camino Way,
footprints were there's no other,
they are just markers of your steps,
they fade, there is no Way,

Dreams of the way,
You are going further,
Your reflection on a lake,
It all just fades to nothing,
like wake trails to the shore.

Like a stone cast into the water,
watching the wake trails fade.
Then, looking back on that path, you may,
the footprints made are gone.

Pilgrim,
There is no other, there is no way,
Only wake trails to the water
All fades away; All fades away.

CHAPTER 8.

THE WAY REVISITED

At this point in the discussion, it's an opportune time to promote my website, caminoway.com.au. Over the past decade, it has proven to be a valuable source for pilgrims on all things Camino.

The Camino is often seen as a journey of self-discovery and spiritual growth. Exploring these aspects could reveal the profound messages that resonate with travellers. While the sources uncovered on the World Wide Web may directly answer why pilgrims are attracted to The Way, they suggest that the caminoway.-com.au website aims to provide travellers with resources to enhance their Camino experience.

My vision at the time implies that in my founding, the website, the Camino, holds significance beyond a mere physical journey. I created the site after my return from the first Camino pilgrimage in 2013. It has always utilised several promotional strategies to attract Camino Way travellers, primarily providing valuable information and resources while promoting its products and services.

The website offers valuable content aimed at Camino Way travellers, including tips for walkers, packing lists, and information on travel packages. caminoway.com.au promotes a range of products and services related to the Camino Way, including books, CDs, and travel packages. These products are presented as valuable resources for travellers to generate revenue and establish the website as a one-stop shop for Camino Way needs. For instance, the website highlights its collection of Camino Way myths, songs, poetry and CDs featuring Camino-themed music, appealing to travellers seeking to enhance their journey with cultural and artistic experiences. Additionally, the website emphasises its travel package deals, offering travellers the convenience of pre-planned itineraries and potentially competitive pricing.

I encourage the reader to check it out. The website fosters engagement with the Camino Way community through its social media presence. This strategy aims to foster a sense of belonging and shared experience among travellers, potentially leading to word-of-mouth marketing and increased website traffic. The website's promotional strategies combine content marketing, product promotion, and community building to attract Camino Way travellers. It does not, however, give answers to the pilgrim on The Way from a spiritual aspect. Walt Whitman once stated in his comments of pilgrims in a world of seekers::" "Not I…nor anyone else can travel that road for you; you must travel it yourself. "

So, why have pilgrims walked the Camino de Santiago Way for over 1,000 years and still do? Some like to take a long walk, while others may pursue spiritual quests, as we have attempted to unfold in previous chapters. Still, others may be on the road, figuring something out, seeking guidance and healing. Everyone has their particular reasons. One may be seeking new vision, companionship, or insight. It soon becomes known to all who tread the weary pathway to Santiago that the traveller, the pilgrim, cannot find deep meaning in their journey until they encounter what is truly sacred.

Anyone would undertake the search if they were not sunk in the everydayness of their life. To become aware of the possibility of the search is to be on to something. Not to be on to something is to be in despair.

The Camino Santiago began on the heels of the reported journey of St. James, who came to Spain after Christ's death to preach that 'faith without works is dead.' The Camino life, like that of Christ, is a journey. Jesus said, ' They who do the will. They who do the will of the Father shall know...." and St. Gregory, "whoever would understand what he hears, must hasten to put into practice what he has heard..." Therefore, please do not wait for great strength before starting: one has to walk towards the light. Are you strong enough to take this first step? Sufficient courage to accomplish a little tiny act of fidelity of reparation, the necessity of which is apparent to you?

Take this step! O, Perform this act! You will be astonished to feel that the effort accomplished, instead of having exhausted your strength, has doubled and that you already see more clearly what you must do next.

For all my depression and apparent lack of strength on my last Camino, I come away with more vitality than ever as a result. I walked through wind and rain, soaked wet for most days and nights, and survived the severe flu. It was nearly 1200 km that I had walked, and I came back to write two new books centred around my Camino journeys and another two albums of songs. If you step out and take the chance to see what may be, you will always gain unexpected joys to overcome pain and discomfort; if I can walk The Way, anyone can do it.

A pilgrim's experience of enduring physical challenges like crossing mountain ranges, traversing valley floors and rocky roads, sandy deserts, and battling the elements of wind and rain may lead to profound spiritual growth and self-discovery. This arduous journey can catalyse a shift in perspective, leading the pilgrim to re-evaluate priorities and find deeper meaning in life beyond material pursuits.

The pilgrim's willingness to endure hardship may stem from a desire to let go of past pain and suffering and seek solace and answers beyond the material world. This process can lead to a reconnection with a higher power or a newfound understanding of their spiritual essence.

The pilgrim may embrace solitude as a means of introspection and self-reflection, finding peace amidst the challenges they face. As they persevere through these trials, pilgrims may discover a wellspring of creativity and a renewed sense of purpose to serve others.

Walk the Way or meditate in seclusion like a hermit cultivates awareness. Mindfulness is being present, recognising one's thoughts and feelings, and responding to life's challenges with clarity and intention. It can be achieved through meditation, prayer, or mindful engagement with daily activities. Mindfulness recognises that life constantly evolves and that clinging to rigid expectations can lead to suffering. The thinking process involves a willingness to adapt to new circumstances and find meaning in the unexpected twists and turns of the journey.

It is making choices aligned with one's values and striving to live in a way that reflects compassion, honesty, and a commitment to personal growth. So, one's action may involve service to others, creative expression, or simply showing up authentically in one's relationships and daily life.

A portrayal of the hermit's retreat is not a rejection of reality but a strategic withdrawal to cultivate inner peace and clarity. Retreating from the world allows the individual to return to the world with a renewed sense of purpose and a desire to contribute meaningfully to society. Through my Camino journeys, for example, I channel my experiences with solitude into creative expression, using writing and music to inspire and support others.

The Camino, with its diverse landscapes, historical significance, and encounters with fellow pilgrims, provides a rich tapestry of experiences to draw upon in creative work. The physical challenge of the journey, the moments of quiet reflection, and the camaraderie forged with fellow travellers all found their way into writing and music, imbuing in works with a sense of authenticity and depth.

The masters of the past, the mystics, emphasise living in the world but not being consumed by its values and expectations. The way, as stated, involves, and I am repeating myself here, discernment and detachment, prioritising spiritual growth and service over the pursuit of material wealth and societal approval. While acknowledging the challenges of this balance, this author strives to embody this principle in his life, seeking to find meaning and purpose beyond the trappings of the material world. I acknowledge that modern technology can facilitate a hermit-like existence without physical participation.

Beyond providing direct inspiration for my work, the Camino is a powerful metaphor in my writing. I frequently use the imagery of the journey to represent the broader human experience, exploring themes of personal transformation, spiritual seeking, and the challenges and rewards of navigating life's unpredictable path.

The Camino experiences were pivotal in shaping my creative journey. The journeys provided a spark of inspiration, a wellspring of material, and a powerful metaphor for exploring the complexities of human experience. The Camino's impact is evident in my creative output's volume and thematic focus, solidifying its place as a transformative force in my life and work. I am proud of my achievements here, but I want to emphasise that much creative thought inspired by my journeys is now pouring in as much to help others as it is to help myself.

The sentiment that "action speaks louder than words," often attributed to St. James, resonates deeply with the experiences of modern-day pilgrims on both the physical Camino de Santiago and the symbolic journey of recovery within Alcoholics Anonymous. The sources, primarily through my account, offer insight into how this principle manifests in both contexts. The Camino de Santiago is intrinsically linked to St. James, the apostle who, according to tradition, preached the message that "faith without works is dead." This message, emphasising the importance of action over mere belief, forms the bedrock of the Camino experience. Pilgrims are not merely retracing St. James's footsteps; they embody his message through walking, enduring hardships, and pushing their limits. The journey becomes an external manifestation of their inner commitment to growth and transformation.

For many pilgrims, the Camino is not just a physical journey but a deeply personal and introspective experience. The message of The Way highlights how the Camino leads individuals from "despair to hope, depression to a progressive recovery to health of body, mind and spirit." This inward journey involves confronting personal demons, shedding layers of self-deception, and embracing vulnerability, as described in my books. The very act of walking, day after day, fosters a meditative state, allowing for deep reflection, embodies the principles of St. James's message, and the Camino finds a parallel in the 12 Steps of Alcoholics Anonymous. As outlined in the Big Book of AA, the steps emphasise the importance of concrete actions to achieve lasting recovery. It's not enough to acknowledge one's powerlessness over alcohol or to inventory one's shortcomings mentally; the Steps demand action: making amends, changing behaviours, and seeking spiritual growth through prayer and meditation .on and reassessing priorities. This internal shift, often sparked by the challenges of the Camino, requires action, not just passive contemplation.

The Steps require active introspection, honesty, and confronting one's flaws and past transgressions. Self-examination is deliberate and often uncomfortable. Equally, the Camino journey is a constant daily progression toward the inner goal of waking up to live a spiritual life.

On the Camino, as in AA, sharing one's inventory with another person requires vulnerability and courage. This concrete action helps break down isolation and shame. It also calls for a willingness to take responsibility for past actions and actively seek reconciliation. The Step involves concrete actions to repair past harms, demonstrating a commitment to change through deeds rather than words.

My Camino experience sparked a creative awakening, leading me to write numerous books and record albums of music. My engagement with the 12 Steps has been instrumental in my ongoing recovery. These achievements are not the result of passive wishing or intellectual understanding; they are the fruits of consistent, deliberate action. The Camino and the AA programs emphasise that the transformation journey is ongoing. The process of inward awakening reminds us that "the hermit's journey is not always clear-cut. He must acknowledge that it is an ongoing process of growth and refinement, of acknowledging imperfections, and of embracing the multifaceted nature of the human experience." This ongoing process necessitates continued action, a commitment to daily practice, self-reflection, and service to others.

The Camino journey, with its unique blend of physical challenge, reflective space, and supportive community, offers a powerful opportunity for individuals to spark a new direction and unlock their creative potential. By embracing the challenges, surrendering to the present moment, and connecting with the deeper meaning of the journey, individuals can emerge transformed, equipped with the insights, experiences, and confidence to pursue their creative passions and live a more fulfilling life.

The Camino de Santiago and awakening to a higher power through the 12 Steps offer parallel paths towards spiritual transformation. Both involve a journey of surrender, introspection, action, connection, and a deepening relationship with a power greater than oneself. While the Camino provides a physical and symbolic framework for this journey, the 12 Steps offer a structured recovery and spiritual growth program. As my account exemplifies, these two paths can intertwine, creating a powerful interaction that leads to lasting change and a more meaningful life.

While the means to an end of spiritual growth for the pilgrims and the Hermit don't focus on physical objects of devotion, they reveal how the Camino de Santiago, the 12 Steps of AA, and the concept of a Higher Power can become profound focal points for faith and spiritual practice. The Camino itself, with its physical and symbolic significance, becomes an object of devotion, embodying the pilgrim's commitment and surrender. The 12 Steps provide a structured framework for spiritual growth and devotion to a Higher Power. At the same time, the concept of a Higher Power, understood individually, acts as a source of transformation and hope. My journey exemplifies how these paths can intersect, creating a powerful interaction that leads to lasting change and a more profound connection to the divine.

CHAPTER 9.

THE OBJECT OF DEVOTION

It is not important what a person's beginning idea of God is and that it develops sufficiently to awaken the devotion necessary to penetrate those levels of consciousness. Herein lie the significant obstacles to the perception and experience of a supra-personal reality.

We have seen that several fields of knowledge point to a transcendent and immanent reality. An approach to such a conviction, as we have said before, can be made through the presumptions of reason, the processes of history, the implication of science, the mystical insights into nature and art, the exploration of dreams through the lives of those who seem to some as the personal manifestation of God. The material assessable here gives only the barest hint of what has been glimpsed using those approaches. Such selection presents only a small position of the author's complete insight. What has been included is hoped to help deepen and extend the reader's sense of ultimate reality.

For some readers, these statements of the objects of devotion may seem meaningless and confusing. Such reasons need not keep the sincere seeker from following The Way, for as Henry Nelson Wieman wrote: " People who live this way have diverse ideas of God, and some seem to have scarcely any idea of God at all."Those conditioned against all ideas of God may use whatever seems worthwhile, whether "Truth, love, simplicity," or being permanent or valuable. Such value can be the opening wedge of devotion.

In research, we have discovered four significant pieces of advice for our approach concerning the Object of Devotion that no idea, nor yet ideas of God, can approximate the actual Reality that men seek- that the ideas are mere fragments of a Whole, mere clues to the ultimate nature of the Good. In this area, more than any other, words used to express ideas should be considered symbols only and kept distinct from the actual reality they attempt to describe. Secondly, no idea should be held on or clung to as final, but rather should be ready to have his particular idea of God' smashed to bits… to, in an instant, find God… For God is the destroyer of Gods. Third, some ideas, explained as animal behavioural implications, block expanding on the cosmology of the Big Bang theory or the base version of astronomy handicap a growing perception of God. Fourth, those who progress beyond dismiss all ideas of God as such, for their experience transcends any rational concept. As Meister Eckhart wrote, "The intellect is no more content with the idea of God than it would be with stone or a tree. It can never rest until it gets to the core of the matter, crashing through to which is beyond the idea of God and truth until it reaches the principle, the beginning of beginnings, the origin or source of all goodness and truth," and as a modern philosopher expressed it:

" No true idea of God in religion may land on; the true idea may constitute a whole which keeps God out, it is adopted as an idea simply, that is to say, as a repetition of other men's insights, as a universal idea, God, who is truly said to explain man to himself, must explain me to me. I must find a god: "This is what I have wanted; this is what I have been meaning all the time; the world as we now see it is a world which can completely live and breathe." It is the way the mystic is trying to make plain- that the idea, as a universe, is insufficient for any man to live by.

"Hence, the chief burden of revelation {as of ideas of a never resting conscience} is that religion must be experience and not as an idea only. There is nothing in the sensation that physical science cannot exhaust except the experience of having sensation. In the same way, nothing in the thematic experience is not expressible in the idea except the experience itself. Herein is the chief part of mystic knowledge, which cannot be otherwise known. Only then is mystic experience possible. Monotonously and age after age, men rediscovered and renounced this never-changing truth as if they were calling on men to exist, live, and save their souls. And what is it to (and what follows from it)? From this point of view, the reiteration of the mystic is justified," save one's soul, if not to be original in this sense. And what follows from it)?

The sources consider the object of devotion in light of the inevitability of loss—through death, departure, or decay—and emphasise the importance of shifting one's focus from the temporal to the eternal. The Object of Devotion explores the journey of a man who, after experiencing profound loss and disillusionment with worldly pursuits, turns inward to seek solace and meaning in connection with a higher power.

It was inevitable that I turned back to the ways of my religious conditioning from childhood to adulthood, initially clinging to conventional religious structures, to eventually embracing a more undefined concept of God, surrendering to a force greater than myself and trusting in its guidance. This inward journey is likened to the experiences of hermits and anchorites, individuals who sought spiritual solitude to deepen their connection with the divine. I recall and recount my experiences on the Camino de Santiago, a pilgrimage to find a symbolic representation of his inner "Sword of Discernment".

Through this arduous journey, I experienced a creative awakening, discovering the ability to express my spiritual insights through poetry, songs, and writing. Subsequent pilgrimages revealed that replacing worldly pursuits with romantic love does not lead to lasting fulfilment. I was forced to confront my ego and return to a path of genuine spiritual seeking.

Ultimately, the source suggests that actual objects of devotion are not found in fleeting external things but in cultivating a spiritual connection that transcends the material world. It means going to the depths of one's consciousness, confronting one's shadows, accepting human nature's complexities, and embracing growth and transformation.

True freedom, like that experienced by hermits and anchorites, lies in aligning oneself with the flow of life, guided by the principles of non-attachment, acceptance, and a willingness to "walk on" in the face of impermanence. Therefore, when faced with the inevitable loss of loved ones and cherished possessions, the mystics suggest that the object of devotion should be shifted from the temporal to the eternal— from the things that crumble to dust to the enduring spiritual connection that provides meaning and purpose. The hermit, or recluse, to work on the inner self involves a continual process of self-discovery, surrender, and cultivating a deep and abiding faith in a power greater than oneself.

Mystical advice offers a multifaceted perspective on pursuing inner peace and harmony, drawing upon personal experiences and insights from various spiritual practices. While acknowledging the potential benefits of selflessly serving others, the mystical masters emphasise cultivating a deep connection with a higher power as the primary source of lasting peace, as does the Steps of Alcoholics Anonymous.

The author recounts his journey of recovery from alcoholism, highlighting the transformative power of the AA program, particularly its emphasis on surrendering to a higher power and embracing spiritual principles.

The author further emphasises this process of surrender and acceptance in his exploration of meditation and prayer. These practices are presented as essential tools for deepening one's connection with the divine and fostering inner transformation. The mystics of old also suggested that creative expression can be a valuable pathway to inner peace. The author's experiences on the Camino de Santiago sparked a creative awakening, leading him to express his spiritual insights through poetry, songs, and writing.

However, it is cautioned that the pursuit of creative output should not be driven by ego or the desire for recognition. Instead, it should be approached as a form of spiritual service, offering one's talents for the benefit of others. My mystic research acknowledges the challenges and complexities of the spiritual journey, highlighting the need for ongoing self-reflection, honesty, and a willingness to confront one's limitations.

The author's struggles with Step 3 of the AA program demonstrate the difficulty of fully surrendering to God's will, especially when confronted with ingrained character defects. AA traditions also emphasise the importance of balancing self-promotion with the principles of anonymity, particularly within the AA fellowship. The sources provide several insights into the nature of inner peace and harmony.

The author reflects on "being in the world but not of it," suggesting that true peace comes from detachment from worldly pursuits and a focus on spirituality. But how does one resonate with the principles of non-attachment and acceptance found in Eastern philosophies such as Buddhism and Taoism?

My research on the objects of devotion also emphasises the importance of embracing the present moment and surrendering to the flow of life rather than clinging to fixed desires or resisting change. Ultimately, the Masters suggest that the path to inner peace and harmony lies in spiritual practices, creative expression, and commitment to self-awareness and growth. While putting others before oneself can be a valuable expression of spiritual principles, the sources prioritise cultivating a deep connection with a higher power as the foundation for lasting peace.

I have explored a personal journey of faith and creativity, drawing upon elements of Christianity and Eastern philosophies. Awakening from this are insights into modern ideas of God as reflected in my former writings herein.

It has come to me as a shift from traditional religious structures to a more personal understanding of God as an "undefinable Godhead." The author moves away from rigid dogma and towards a more intuitive, experiential connection with the divine. This resonates with contemporary spiritual movements that emphasise personal experience over institutionalised religion.

My retreat to a "cave" symbolises a search for meaning and purpose in solitude. Thus, it echoes the historical practice of hermits and anchorites who sought spiritual enlightenment through isolation and contemplation. These writings suggest that even in modern society, solitude can be a powerful tool for connecting with a higher power. So it has come to pass that I have experienced a creative awakening during my time of spiritual seeking, finding that the "dragon's mouth" of despair transformed into a "lotus flower of creative ideas". Thus, it suggests a link between the divine and the creative impulse, aligning with the belief that artistic inspiration can be a conduit for spiritual insight.

It is a struggle for me to surrender to God's will in a total personal surrender. I struggle with the concept of surrendering to God's will, particularly within the framework of the Alcoholics Anonymous Twelve Steps. A reflection of a common challenge in modern spirituality is reconciling personal agency with believing in a higher power. I can only rely on contemplation prayer as an ongoing process of surrendering to God's plan, which involves more self-reflection, humility, and a willingness to change.

Some years ago, my counsellor had enquired if I still practised the faith of my childhood. When I replied that I did not in the traditional sense, he remarked that it was a pity as the Catholic religion is an excellent source of guidance through symbolism. He emphasises the importance of symbols in religious experience, arguing that they can reveal more profound truths about ourselves and the world. This aligns with the work of Carl Jung, who saw symbols as expressions of the collective unconscious. Lately, I've been paying more attention to suggestions that symbols, whether in dreams, art, or religious rituals, help my connection with the divine.

I still wrestle with the tension between this hermit's desire for solitude and the call to serve others. Integrating personal growth with social responsibility is a broader challenge in contemporary spirituality. Service to others can be a form of spiritual practice, even when pursued within a solitary path.

The Master sources of my introspection here present a personal interpretation of God, emphasising experience, intuition, and the transformative power of self-discovery. My journey thus far highlights how modern individuals can seek and connect with the divine, even amidst the complexities and challenges of contemporary life.

In concluding this chapter on the object of devotion, it seems the most important thing is to accept God as a guiding force and stop trying to define him. It appears to be now a simple opening of myself to whatever comes, trusting in God's plan for me. It was always thus in my childhood; somehow, I lost that faith and trust along the way. Also, to maintain sobriety, I must practice the principles of AA in all my daily affairs. The recovery programme of AA includes being honest with yourself, being open-minded, being willing to grow, not worrying, being accepting, and believing in living with whatever comes your way.

Most importantly, we should try to live in the world but not be of it. We should also be mindful of the dangers of worldly desires, such as fame, fortune, and romantic relationships, which can lead to pain and suffering.

Instead, I need to focus more on spiritual growth and service to God and others, using the Steps of the AA programme as my guiding influence and maintaining serenity in a hermit's lifestyle in my private life. Daily committing to practising prayer and meditation is a good way to start. In this daily plan of action, I can be mindful of my thoughts and actions throughout the day.

I am assured that as I do these things, I will develop a deeper connection with God and a greater understanding of His will for my life. It also helps to talk to others in AA who practice these principles in their affairs. They are great friends who offer support and guidance as I work to rekindle my connection to God, my object of devotion, and live a more spiritual life.

CHAPTER 10

EPILOGUE

I was like a blind man crossing the Spanish Masada. I had crossed its one-hundred-kilometre distance twice before. Once amid a forty-two-degree summer heatwave on a dusty, sandy track and another in an autumn of constant rain, wind and slushy mud. My life was a little like both of those problematic spiritual trudges. In such a mind, I wrote a poem to contemplate my present-day dilemma and meditatively come to terms with the inner spirit. I was searching for love and found a shadow from which I was searching in the embrace of another woman's body. Her lust was just as ravaging and damaging as my own. It never did work out on that Camino journey, for, in essence, my searching led me to lust, not love—a place where God is not, at least not for me.

The content of this book does not explicitly discuss the concept of love in the context of what psychology and the Step work of AA suggest, nor does it provide the depth of Christ's sacrifice and its potential benefits. However, it offers insights into the author's spiritual journey, which can be used to examine the idea of love as a driving force for selflessness and growth.

The book focuses on the author's quest for meaning and purpose. He confronts his inner demons and seeks a deeper connection with a higher power. His journey is characterised by periods of isolation, introspection, and a willingness to let go of worldly attachments. This process aligns with the idea of sacrificing worldly pursuits for spiritual growth, echoing Christ's sacrifice for humanity.

The physical and emotional challenges of the Camino de Santiago symbolise the difficulties encountered on any path of personal transformation. The author's perseverance through hardship and interactions with fellow pilgrims can be seen as acts of love – love for himself, the journey, and those he encounters. His willingness to embrace the unknown and step outside his comfort zone reflects the selflessness often associated with love.

Ultimately, the Camino journey and that of a hermit suggest that true fulfilment involves finding a balance between solitude and connection, integrating the insights gained through introspection into a life of service and engagement with others.

I reflect on the concept of "serving and being served," recognising the interconnectedness of humanity and the importance of contributing to something larger than oneself. It resonates with love as a selfless service, where personal growth and fulfilment are achieved through giving to others. In the time of the author's hermit-like isolation, both in a literal cave and in his modern-day life, the book emphasises the importance of solitude for introspection and spiritual growth. This withdrawal from the world can be seen as another form of self-sacrifice, allowing for a deeper connection with the inner self and, by extension, a greater capacity for love and compassion.

While the book does not directly address the action of love from a Christ-like perspective of sacrifice, my journey offers valuable insights [for me as well as you, the reader] into the themes of self-discovery, sacrifice, service, and solitude—all of which are relevant to understanding love as a transformative force. Further exploration of theological and philosophical texts may be needed to understand this complex topic comprehensively.

In contemplating how to conclude this book, poetic self-expression would be the best way to summarise it.

The Crossing

Each word a sip of water
Near the mouth of men
Silence is the sound
Of meditation.

All you feel is walking,
All you hear
The sound of feet
You are not thirsty now.

There is just a sound.
Like a whisper
In the wind,
Like ice under one's feet.

You are not here yourself.
Moved to another world,
You are not here yourself,
Moved to another world.

You are in the crossing,
Hear the sound of your own feet
Upon the journey
You are on the Way.

It is dark now
Your headlamp be
Your only friend
Lights the tunnel of your Way.

A blind man crossing new borders,
He carries his knapsack,
Crossing the borders
Of the Way.

You are not here yourself,
Moved to another world,
you are not here yourself,
Moved to another world.

The noise is deafening,
Thunder & rain
You are a grain of sand
You are on the beach.

The storm is over now,
It is a new day,
You were in the abyss,
But now you see the Way.

There is always light.
In the darkest hour,
Pilgrim's eyes are opening
The void is deafening.

You were not here yourself,
Moving to another world
You are here now yourself,
Moving back into the world.

After completing my third album of songs and yet another book, I wondered what I could gain from my creative outpourings. I've turned this poem into a song, which more or less sums up my feelings about my life and where I am along the road to salvation.

The reference to hack has more to do with penning a line of rhyme than with any journalistic skills I possess. It is more about facing fact than the fiction of hiding in the shadow of self. It speaks of my limitations and my genuine, heartfelt desire. It's called an Old Bush Hack.

Well, I'm an old bush hack.
With a knapsack on my back
I've no work now
No money for my pride.

And I've tried my hand at busking
Selling songs and books outback
I've no place to call my home
And that's a fact.

I did time in the shearing sheds
Branding cattle, drenching sheep
It's a hard life on the road
And that's a fact.

So I carry my books
For insurance
CDs of the songs
That I wrote,

For a dollar or two
I'll sell you the bloom'en lot
But my backpack and sleeping sack
Are worth their weight in gold

So, I'll not be selling you that
No, I'll not be selling you that!

Well, I tried my hand at busking
So many songs I sang
 at the country music shows
A one-person band

There's no money in the life.
Of a country music man
And authors are a dying breed
As any fool would know

Oh! It's no stable life.
No one to call my own
When love's do come
They will surely go

So I carry my books
for insurance
CDs of the songs
That I wrote

For a dollar or two
I'll sell you the bloom'en lot,
But my backpack and sleeping sack
Are worth their weight in gold

So, I'll not be selling you that
No, I'm not selling you that!

Well, I'm an old bush hack,
With a knapsack on my back
I've no work now
No money for my pride

And I've tried my hand at busking
Selling songs and books outback
I've no place to call my own
And that's a fact!

So I'm on the frog and toad
With a knapsack on my back
I'm heading for someplace
I've never been.

Twelve Steps of Alcoholics Anonymous will see these Promises come true:

Promise 1: We will have new freedom and happiness.

Promise 2: We will not regret the past nor wish to shut the door on it.

Promise 3: We will comprehend the word serenity.

Promise 4: We will know peace.

Promise 5: No matter how far down the scale we have gone, we will see how our experience can benefit others.

Promise 6: The feeling of uselessness and self-pity will disappear.

Promise 7: We will lose interest in selfish things and gain interest in our fellows.

Promise 8: Self-seeking will slip away.

Promise 9: Our whole attitude and outlook upon life will change.

Promise 10: Fear of people and economic insecurity will leave us.

Promise 11: We will intuitively know how to handle situations that used to baffle us.

Promise 12: We will suddenly realise that God is doing what we could not do for ourselves.

About the Author.

Doug McPhillips, poet, singer, songwriter, and author, began his journey of discovery over a decade ago after having had life-changing experiences.

The many tracks he has traversed through the Northern Hemisphere and down under in Australia and New Zealand have resulted in the facts and fiction of this novel.

Doug has recorded and sung songs interrelated to his many works, with mystic melodies in an authentic Australian style.

Doug has written several novels, two books of poems, a travel guide and three albums of his songs, all inspired by his adventurers.

Doug is an adventurer who divides his time between family and friends, his creative pursuits, and those who benefit most from his efforts and experience.

Reference material for this book includes:

Alcoholics Anonymous, 4th Edition AA World Service, 1976

As Bill sees it. 18th Print, AA World Service. 2017.

Daily Reflections, 11th print, AA World Service. 2014.

Journey to the Inner Mountain, Hodder & Staughton, James Cowan, 2002.

The Choice is Always Ours, Jove Publications.1997

Santiago Traveller: Ingram Sparke, Doug McPhillips. 2018

References of Authors within the content of this book.

NotebookLM and ty the use of Artificial Intelligence.

Google Research from Authors unknown.